James Baldwin

VINTAGE **BALDWIN**

James Baldwin was born in 1924 and educated in New York. He is the author of more than twenty works of fiction and nonfiction, including *Go Tell It on the Mountain*; *Notes of a Native Son*; *Giovanni's Room*; *Nobody Knows My Name*; *Another Country*; *The Fire Next Time*; *Nothing Personal*; *Blues for Mister Charlie*; *Going to Meet the Man*; *The Amen Corner*; *Tell Me How Long the Train's Been Gone*; *One Day When I Was Lost*; *No Name in the Street*; *If Beale Street Could Talk*; *The Devil Finds Work*; *Little Man, Little Man*; *Just Above My Head*; *The Evidence of Things Not Seen*; *Jimmy's Blues*; and *The Price of the Ticket*. Among the awards he received are a Eugene F. Saxon Memorial Trust Award, a Rosenwald Fellowship, a Guggenheim Fellowship, a *Partisan Review* Fellowship, and a Ford Foundation grant. He was made a Commander of the Legion of Honor in 1986. He died in 1987.

Go Tell It on the Mountain
Notes of a Native Son
Giovanni's Room
Nobody Knows My Name
Another Country
The Fire Next Time
Nothing Personal
Blues for Mister Charlie
Going to Meet the Man
The Amen Corner
Tell Me How Long the Train's Been Gone
One Day When I Was Lost
No Name in the Street
If Beale Street Could Talk
The Devil Finds Work
Little Man, Little Man
Just Above My Head
The Evidence of Things Not Seen
Jimmy's Blues
The Price of the Ticket

VINTAGE BALDWIN

James Baldwin

VINTAGE BOOKS

A Division of Random House, Inc.

New York

A VINTAGE ORIGINAL, JANUARY 2004

Copyright © 2004 by The Estate of James Baldwin

"My Dungeon Shook" was published in *The Fire Next Time* copyright © 1962, 1963
by James Baldwin, copyright renewed 1990, 1991 by Gloria Baldwin Karefa-Smart
(Vintage Books, 1993). "Fifth Avenue, Uptown: A Letter from Harlem,"
"Nobody Knows My Name: A Letter from the South," and "The Discovery of
What It Means to Be an American" were originally published in *Nobody Knows My
Name* copyright © 1954, 1956, 1958, 1959, 1960, 1961 by James Baldwin, copyright
renewed 1988, 1989 by Gloria Baldwin Karefa-Smart (Vintage Books, 1993).
"Sonny's Blues" was originally published in *Going to Meet the Man* copyright © 1948,
1951, 1957, 1958, 1960, 1965 by James Baldwin, copyright renewed 1993 by The
Estate of James Baldwin (Vintage Books, 1995). Selection from *Another Country*
was originally published in *Another Country* copyright © 1960, 1962 by James
Baldwin, copyright renewed 1988, 1990 by Gloria Baldwin Karefa-Smart (Vintage
Books, 1993). Notes for *The Amen Corner* and "The Next Morning": Act III were
originally published in *The Amen Corner* copyright © 1968 by James Baldwin,
copyright renewed 1996 by The Estate of James Baldwin (Vintage Books, 1998).

Library of Congress Cataloging-in-Publication Data
Baldwin, James.
Vintage Baldwin / James Baldwin
1st Vintage Books ed.
p.   cm.
ISBN 978-1-4000-3394-2
1. African Americans—Fiction.   2. African Americans.
PS3552.A45 A6 2004
813'.54—dc 22
2003057566

Book design by JoAnne Metsch

www.vintagebooks.com

CONTENTS

VINTAGE BALDWIN

MY DUNGEON SHOOK:
Letter to My Nephew on the One Hundredth Anniversary of the Emancipation

Dear James:

I have begun this letter five times and torn it up five times. I keep seeing your face, which is also the face of your father and my brother. Like him, you are tough, dark, vulnerable, moody—with a very definite tendency to sound truculent because you want no one to think you are soft. You may be like your grandfather in this, I don't know, but certainly both you and your father resemble him very much physically. Well, he is dead, he never saw you, and he had a terrible life; he was defeated long before he died because, at the bottom of his heart, he really believed what white people said about him. This is one of the reasons that he became so holy. I am sure that your father has told you something about all that. Neither you nor your father exhibit any tendency towards holiness: you really *are* of another era, part of what happened when the Negro left the land and came into what the late E. Franklin Frazier called "the cities of destruction." You can only be destroyed by believing that you really are what the white world calls a *nigger.* I tell you this because I love you, and please don't you ever forget it.

I have known both of you all your lives, have carried your Daddy in my arms and on my shoulders, kissed and spanked him and watched him learn to walk. I don't know if you've known anybody from that far back; if you've loved anybody that long, first as an infant, then as a child, then as a man, you gain a strange perspective on time and human pain and effort. Other people cannot see what I see whenever I look into your father's face, for behind your father's face as it is today are all those other faces which were his. Let him laugh and I see a cellar your father does not remember and a house he does not remember and I hear in his present laughter his laughter as a child. Let him curse and I remember him falling down the cellar steps, and howling, and I remember, with pain, his tears, which my hand or your grandmother's so easily wiped away. But no one's hand can wipe away those tears he sheds invisibly today, which one hears in his laughter and in his speech and in his songs. I know what the world has done to my brother and how narrowly he has survived it. And I know, which is much worse, and this is the crime of which I accuse my country and my countrymen, and for which neither I nor time nor history will ever forgive them, that they have destroyed and are destroying hundreds of thousands of lives and do not know it and do not want to know it. One can be, indeed one must strive to become, tough and philosophical concerning destruction and death, for this is what most of mankind has been best at since we have heard of man. (But remember: *most* of mankind is not *all* of mankind.) But it is not permissible that the authors of devastation should also be innocent. It is the innocence which constitutes the crime.

Now, my dear namesake, these innocent and well-meaning people, your countrymen, have caused you to be born under conditions not very far removed from those described for us by Charles Dickens in the London of more than a hundred years ago. (I hear the chorus of the innocents screaming, "No! This is not true! How *bitter* you are!"—but I am writing this letter to *you,* to try to tell you something about how to handle *them,* for most of them do not yet really know that you exist. I *know* the conditions under which you were born, for I was there. Your countrymen were *not* there, and haven't made it yet. Your grandmother was also there, and no one has ever accused her of being bitter. I suggest that the innocents check with her. She isn't hard to find. Your countrymen don't know that *she* exists, either, though she has been working for them all their lives.)

Well, you were born, here you came, something like fifteen years ago; and though your father and mother and grandmother, looking about the streets through which they were carrying you, staring at the walls into which they brought you, had every reason to be heavyhearted, yet they were not. For here you were, Big James, named for me—you were a big baby, I was not—here you were: to be loved. To be loved, baby, hard, at once, and forever, to strengthen you against the loveless world. Remember that: I know how black it looks today, for you. It looked bad that day, too, yes, we were trembling. We have not stopped trembling yet, but if we had not loved each other none of us would have survived. And now you must survive because we love you, and for the sake of your children and your children's children.

This innocent country set you down in a ghetto in which, in fact, it intended that you should perish. Let me spell out precisely what I mean by that, for the heart of the matter is here, and the root of my dispute with my country. You were born where you were born and faced the future that you faced because you were black and *for no other reason*. The limits of your ambition were, thus, expected to be set forever. You were born into a society which spelled out with brutal clarity, and in as many ways as possible, that you were a worthless human being. You were not expected to aspire to excellence: you were expected to make peace with mediocrity. Wherever you have turned, James, in your short time on this earth, you have been told where you could go and what you could do (and *how* you could do it) and where you could live and whom you could marry. I know your countrymen do not agree with me about this, and I hear them saying, "You exaggerate." They do not know Harlem, and I do. So do you. Take no one's word for anything, including mine—but trust your experience. Know whence you came. If you know whence you came, there is really no limit to where you can go. The details and symbols of your life have been deliberately constructed to make you believe what white people say about you. Please try to remember that what they believe, as well as what they do and cause you to endure, does not testify to your inferiority but to their inhumanity and fear. Please try to be clear, dear James, through the storm which rages about your youthful head today, about the reality which lies behind the words *acceptance* and *integration*. There is no reason for you to try to become like white people and there is no basis whatever for their impertinent assumption that *they* must accept *you*. The really terrible thing, old buddy, is that *you* must accept *them*. And I mean that very seriously. You must accept them and accept them with love. For these innocent people have no other hope.

They are, in effect, still trapped in a history which they do not understand; and until they understand it, they cannot be released from it. They have had to believe for many years, and for innumerable reasons, that black men are inferior to white men. Many of them, indeed, know better, but, as you will discover, people find it very difficult to act on what they know. To act is to be committed, and to be committed is to be in danger. In this case, the danger, in the minds of most white Americans, is the loss of their identity. Try to imagine how you would feel if you woke up one morning to find the sun shining and all the stars aflame. You would be frightened because it is out of the order of nature. Any upheaval in the universe is terrifying because it so profoundly attacks one's sense of one's own reality. Well, the black man has functioned in the white man's world as a fixed star, as an immovable pillar: and as he moves out of his place, heaven and earth are shaken to their foundations. You, don't be afraid. I said that it was intended that you should perish in the ghetto, perish by never being allowed to go behind the white man's definitions, by never being allowed to spell your proper name. You have, and many of us have, defeated this intention; and, by a terrible law, a terrible paradox, those innocents who believed that your imprisonment made them safe are losing their grasp of reality. But these men are your brothers—your lost, younger brothers. And if the word *integration* means anything, this is what it means: that we, with love, shall force our brothers to see themselves as they are, to cease fleeing from reality and begin to change it. For this is your home, my friend, do not be driven from it; great men have done great things here, and will again, and we can make America what America must become. It will be hard, James, but you come from sturdy, peasant stock, men who picked cotton and dammed rivers and built railroads, and, in the teeth of the most terrifying odds, achieved an unassailable and monumental dignity. You come from a long line of great poets, some of the greatest poets since Homer. One of them said, *The very time I thought I was lost, My dungeon shook and my chains fell off.*

You know, and I know, that the country is celebrating one hundred years of freedom one hundred years too soon. We cannot be free until they are free. God bless you, James, and Godspeed.

Your uncle,
James

There is a housing project standing now where the house in which we grew up once stood, and one of those stunted city trees is snarling where our doorway used to be. This is on the rehabilitated side of the avenue. The other side of the avenue—for progress takes time—has not been rehabilitated yet and it looks exactly as it looked in the days when we sat with our noses pressed against the windowpane, longing to be allowed to go "across the street." The grocery store which gave us credit is still there, and there can be no doubt that it is still giving credit. The people in the project certainly need it—far more, indeed, than they ever needed the project. The last time I passed by, the Jewish proprietor was still standing among his shelves, looking sadder and heavier but scarcely any older. Farther down the block stands the shoe-repair store in which our shoes were repaired until reparation became impossible and in which, then, we bought all our "new" ones. The Negro proprietor is still in the window, head down, working at the leather.

These two, I imagine, could tell a long tale if they would (perhaps they would be glad to if they could), having watched so many, for so long, struggling in the fish-hooks, the barbed wire, of this avenue.

The avenue is elsewhere the renowned and elegant Fifth. The area I am describing, which, in today's gang parlance, would be called "the turf," is bounded by Lenox Avenue on the west, the Harlem River on the east, 135th Street on the north, and 130th Street on the south. We never lived beyond these boundaries; this is where we grew up. Walking along 145th Street—for example—familiar as it is, and similar, does not have the same impact because I do not know any of the people on the block. But when I turn east on 131st Street and Lenox Avenue, there is first a soda-pop joint, then a shoeshine "parlor," then a grocery store, then a dry cleaners', then the houses. All along the street there are people who watched me grow up, people who grew up with me, people I watched grow up along with my brothers and sisters; and, sometimes in my arms, sometimes underfoot, sometimes at my shoulder— or on it—their children, a riot, a forest of children, who include my nieces and nephews.

When we reach the end of this long block, we find

ourselves on wide, filthy, hostile Fifth Avenue, facing that project which hangs over the avenue like a monument to the folly, and the cowardice, of good intentions. All along the block, for anyone who knows it, are immense human gaps, like craters. These gaps are not created merely by those who have moved away, inevitably into some other ghetto; or by those who have risen, almost always into a greater capacity for self-loathing and self-delusion; or yet by those who, by whatever means—World War II, the Korean War, a policeman's gun or billy, a gang war, a brawl, madness, an overdose of heroin, or, simply, unnatural exhaustion—are dead. I am talking about those who are left, and I am talking principally about the young. What are they doing? Well, some, a minority, are fanatical churchgoers, members of the more extreme of the Holy Roller sects. Many, many more are "moslems," by affiliation or sympathy, that is to say that they are united by nothing more—and nothing less—than a hatred of the white world and all its works. They are present, for example, at every Buy Black street-corner meeting—meetings in which the speaker urges his hearers to cease trading with white men and establish a separate economy. Neither the speaker nor his hearers can possibly do this, of course, since Negroes do not own General Motors or RCA or the A&P, nor, indeed, do they own more than a wholly insufficient fraction of anything else in Harlem (those who *do* own anything are more interested in their profits than in their fellows). But these meetings nevertheless keep alive in the participators a certain pride of bitterness without which, however futile this bitterness may be, they could scarcely remain alive at all. Many have given up. They stay home and watch the TV screen, living on the earnings of their parents, cousins, brothers, or uncles, and only leave the house to go to the movies or to the nearest bar. "How're you making it?" one may ask, running into them along the block, or in the bar. "Oh, I'm TV-ing it"; with the saddest, sweetest, most shamefaced of smiles, and from a great distance. This distance one is compelled to respect; anyone who has traveled so far will not easily be dragged again into the world. There are further retreats, of course, than the TV screen or the bar. There are those who are simply sitting on their stoops, "stoned," animated for a moment only, and hideously, by the approach of someone who may lend them the money for a "fix." Or by the approach of someone from whom they can purchase it, one of the shrewd ones, on the way to prison or just coming out.

And the others, who have avoided all of these deaths, get up in the morning and go downtown to meet "the man." They work in the white man's world all day and come home in the evening to this fetid block. They struggle to instill in their children some private sense of honor or dignity which will help the child to survive. This means, of course, that they must struggle, stolidly, incessantly, to keep this sense alive in themselves, in spite of the insults,

the indifference, and the cruelty they are certain to encounter in their working day. They patiently browbeat
the landlord into fixing the heat, the plaster, the plumbing;
this demands prodigious patience; nor is patience usually
enough. In trying to make their hovels habitable, they are
perpetually throwing good money after bad. Such frustration, so long endured, is driving many strong, admirable
men and women whose only crime is color to the very
gates of paranoia.

One remembers them from another time—playing
handball in the playground, going to church, wondering
if they were going to be promoted at school. One remembers them going off to war—gladly, to escape this block.
One remembers their return. Perhaps one remembers their
wedding day. And one sees where the girl is now—vainly
looking for salvation from some other embittered, trussed,
and struggling boy—and sees the all-but-abandoned children in the streets.

Now I am perfectly aware that there are other slums in
which white men are fighting for their lives, and mainly
losing. I know that blood is also flowing through those
streets and that the human damage there is incalculable.
People are continually pointing out to me the wretchedness of white people in order to console me for the
wretchedness of blacks. But an itemized account of the
American failure does not console me and it should not
console anyone else. That hundreds of thousands of white

people are living, in effect, no better than the "niggers" is not a fact to be regarded with complacency. The social and moral bankruptcy suggested by this fact is of the bitterest, most terrifying kind.

The people, however, who believe that this democratic anguish has some consoling value are always pointing out that So-and-So, white, and So-and-So, black, rose from the slums into the big time. The existence—the public existence—of, say, Frank Sinatra and Sammy Davis, Jr., proves to them that America is still the land of opportunity and that inequalities vanish before the determined will. It proves nothing of the sort. The determined will is rare— at the moment, in this country, it is unspeakably rare—and the inequalities suffered by the many are in no way justified by the rise of a few. A few have always risen—in every country, every era, and in the teeth of regimes which can by no stretch of the imagination be thought of as free. Not all of these people, it is worth remembering, left the world better than they found it. The determined will is rare, but it is not invariably benevolent. Furthermore, the American equation of success with the big times reveals an awful disrespect for human life and human achievement. This equation has placed our cities among the most dangerous in the world and has placed our youth among the most empty and most bewildered. The situation of our youth is not mysterious. Children have never been very good at listening to their elders, but they have never failed to imitate

them. They must, they have no other models. That is
exactly what our children are doing. They are imitating
our immorality, our disrespect for the pain of others.

All other slum dwellers, when the bank account per-
mits it, can move out of the slum and vanish altogether
from the eye of persecution. No Negro in this country
has ever made that much money and it will be a long time
before any Negro does. The Negroes in Harlem, who
have no money, spend what they have on such gimcracks
as they are sold. These include "wider" TV screens, more
"faithful" hi-fi sets, more "powerful" cars, all of which,
of course, are obsolete long before they are paid for. Anyone who has ever struggled with poverty knows how
extremely expensive it is to be poor; and if one is a member of a captive population, economically speaking, one's
feet have simply been placed on the treadmill forever.
One is victimized, economically, in a thousand ways—
rent, for example, or car insurance. Go shopping one day
in Harlem—for anything—and compare Harlem prices
and quality with those downtown.

The people who have managed to get off this block have
only got as far as a more respectable ghetto. This respectable ghetto does not even have the advantages of the dis-
reputable one—friends, neighbors, a familiar church, and
friendly tradesmen; and it is not, moreover, in the nature
of any ghetto to remain respectable long. Every Sunday,
people who have left the block take the lonely ride back,

dragging their increasingly discontented children with them. They spend the day talking, not always with words, about the trouble they've seen and the trouble—one must watch their eyes as they watch their children—they are only too likely to see. For children do not like ghettos. It takes them nearly no time to discover exactly why they are there.

The projects in Harlem are hated. They are hated almost as much as policemen, and this is saying a great deal. And they are hated for the same reason: both reveal, unbearably, the real attitude of the white world, no matter how many liberal speeches are made, no matter how many lofty editorials are written, no matter how many civil-rights commissions are set up.

The projects are hideous, of course, there being a law, apparently respected throughout the world, that popular housing shall be as cheerless as a prison. They are lumped all over Harlem, colorless, bleak, high, and revolting. The wide windows look out on Harlem's invincible and indescribable squalor: the Park Avenue railroad tracks, around which, about forty years ago, the present dark community began; the unrehabilitated houses, bowed down, it would seem, under the great weight of frustration and bitterness they contain; the dark, the ominous schoolhouses from which the child may emerge maimed, blinded, hooked, or enraged for life; and the churches, churches, block upon block of churches, niched in the walls like cannon in the walls of a fortress. Even if the administration of the projects were not so insanely humiliating (for example: one must report raises in salary to the management, which will then eat up the profit by raising one's rent; the management has the right to know who is staying in your apartment; the management can ask you to leave, at their discretion), the projects would still be hated because they are an insult to the meanest intelligence.

Harlem got its first private project, Riverton*—which is now, naturally, a slum—about twelve years ago because at that time Negroes were not allowed to live in Stuyvesant Town. Harlem watched Riverton go up, therefore, in the most violent bitterness of spirit, and hated it long before the builders arrived. They began hating it at about the time people began moving out of their condemned houses to make room for this additional proof of how thoroughly the white world despised them. And they had

*The inhabitants of Riverton were much embittered by this description; they have, apparently, forgotten how their project came into being; and have repeatedly informed me that I cannot possibly be referring to Riverton, but to another housing project which is directly across the street. It is quite clear, I think, that I have no interest in accusing any individuals or families of the depredations herein described: but neither can I deny the evidence of my own eyes. Nor do I blame anyone in Harlem for making the best of a dreadful bargain. But anyone who lives in Harlem and imagines that he has *not* struck this bargain, or that what he takes to be his status (in whose eyes?) protects him against the common pain, demoralization, and danger, is simply self deluded.

scarcely moved in, naturally, before they began smashing windows, defacing walls, urinating in the elevators, and fornicating in the playgrounds. Liberals, both white and black, were appalled at the spectacle. I was appalled by the liberal innocence—or cynicism, which comes out in practice as much the same thing. Other people were delighted to be able to point to proof positive that nothing could be done to better the lot of the colored people. They were, and are, right in one respect: that nothing can be done as long as they are treated like colored people. The people in Harlem know they are living there because white people do not think they are good enough to live anywhere else. No amount of "improvement" can sweeten this fact. Whatever money is now being earmarked to improve this, or any other ghetto, might as well be burnt. A ghetto can be improved in one way only: out of existence.

Similarly, the only way to police a ghetto is to be oppressive. None of the Police Commissioner's men, even with the best will in the world, have any way of understanding the lives led by the people they swagger about in twos and threes controlling. Their very presence is an insult, and it would be, even if they spent their entire day feeding gumdrops to children. They represent the force of the white world, and that world's real intentions are, simply, for that world's criminal profit and ease, to keep the black man corraled up here, in his place. The badge, the gun in the holster, and the swinging club make vivid what will happen should his rebellion become overt. Rare, indeed, is the Harlem citizen, from the most circumspect church member to the most shiftless adolescent, who does not have a long tale to tell of police incompetence, injustice, or brutality. I myself have witnessed and endured it more than once. The businessmen and racketeers also have a story. And so do the prostitutes. (And this is not, perhaps, the place to discuss Harlem's very complex attitude toward black policemen, nor the reasons, according to Harlem, that they are nearly all downtown.)

It is hard, on the other hand, to blame the policeman, blank, good-natured, thoughtless, and insuperably innocent, for being such a perfect representative of the people he serves. He, too, believes in good intentions and is astounded and offended when they are not taken for the deed. He has never, himself, done anything for which to be hated—which of us has?—and yet he is facing, daily and nightly, people who would gladly see him dead, and he knows it. There is no way for him not to know it: there are few things under heaven more unnerving than the silent, accumulating contempt and hatred of a people. He moves through Harlem, therefore, like an occupying soldier in a bitterly hostile country; which is precisely what, and where, he is, and is the reason he walks in twos and threes. And he is not the only one who knows why he is always in company: the people who are watching him know why, too. Any street meeting, sacred or secular, which he and his colleagues uneasily cover has as its explicit or implicit burden the cruelty and injustice of the white domination. And these days, of course, in terms increasingly vivid and jubilant, it speaks of the end of that domination. The white policeman standing on a Harlem street corner finds himself at the very center of the revolution now occurring in the world. He is not prepared for it—naturally, nobody is—and, what is possibly much more to the point, he is exposed, as few white people are, to the anguish of the black people around him. Even if he is gifted with the merest mustard grain of imagination, something must seep in. He cannot avoid observing that some of the children, in spite of their color, remind him of children he has known and loved, perhaps even of his own children. He knows that he certainly does not want *his* children living this way. He can retreat from his uneasiness in only one direction: into a callousness which very shortly becomes second nature. He becomes more callous, the population becomes more hostile, the situation grows more tense, and the police force is increased. One day, to everyone's astonishment, someone drops a match in the powder keg and everything blows up. Before the dust has settled or the blood congealed, editorials, speeches, and civil-rights commissions are loud in the land, demanding to know what happened. What happened is that Negroes want to be treated like men.

Negroes want to be treated like men: a perfectly straight-

forward statement, containing only seven words. People
who have mastered Kant, Hegel, Shakespeare, Marx, Freud,
and the Bible find this statement utterly impenetrable.
The idea seems to threaten profound, barely conscious
assumptions. A kind of panic paralyzes their features, as
though they found themselves trapped on the edge of a
steep place. I once tried to describe to a very well-known
American intellectual the conditions among Negroes in
the South. My recital disturbed him and made him indig-
nant; and he asked me in perfect innocence, "Why don't
all the Negroes in the South move North?" I tried to
explain what *has* happened, unfailingly, whenever a significant body of Negroes move North. They do not escape
Jim Crow: they merely encounter another, not-less-deadly
variety. They do not move to Chicago, they move to
the South Side; they do not move to New York, they
move to Harlem. The pressure within the ghetto causes
the ghetto walls to expand, and this expansion is always
violent. White people hold the line as long as they can,
and in as many ways as they can, from verbal intimidation
to physical violence. But inevitably the border which has
divided the ghetto from the rest of the world falls into the
hands of the ghetto. The white people fall back bitterly
before the black horde; the landlords make a tidy profit by
raising the rent, chopping up the rooms, and all but dis-
pensing with the upkeep; and what has once been a
neighborhood turns into a "turf." This is precisely what

happened when the Puerto Ricans arrived in their thousands—and the bitterness thus caused is, as I write, being fought out all up and down those streets.

Northerners indulge in an extremely dangerous luxury. They seem to feel that because they fought on the right side during the Civil War, and won, they have earned the right merely to deplore what is going on in the South, without taking any responsibility for it; and that they can ignore what is happening in Northern cities because what is happening in Little Rock or Birmingham is worse. Well, in the first place, it is not possible for anyone who has not endured both to know which is "worse." I know Negroes who prefer the South and white Southerners, because "At least there, you haven't got to play any guessing games!" The guessing games referred to have driven more than one Negro into the narcotics ward, the madhouse, or the river. I know another Negro, a man very dear to me, who says, with conviction and with truth, "The spirit of the South is the spirit of America." He was born in the North and did his military training in the South. He did not, as far as I can gather, find the South "worse"; he found it, if anything, all too familiar. In the second place, though, even if Birmingham *is* worse, no doubt Johannesburg, South Africa, beats it by several miles, and Buchenwald was one of the worst things that ever happened in the entire history of the world. The world has never lacked for horrifying examples; but I do not believe that these examples are meant to be used as justification for our own crimes. This perpetual justification empties the heart of all human feeling. The emptier our hearts become, the greater will be our crimes. Thirdly, the South is not merely an embarrassingly backward region, but a part of this country, and what happens there concerns every one of us.

As far as the color problem is concerned, there is but one great difference between the Southern white and the Northerner: the Southerner remembers, historically and in his own psyche, a kind of Eden in which he loved black people and they loved him. Historically, the flaming sword laid across this Eden is the Civil War. Personally, it is the Southerner's sexual coming of age, when, without any warning, unbreakable taboos are set up between himself and his past. Everything, thereafter, is permitted him except the love he remembers and has never ceased to need. The resulting, indescribable torment affects every Southern mind and is the basis of the Southern hysteria.

None of this is true for the Northerner. Negroes represent nothing to him personally, except, perhaps, the dangers of carnality. He never sees Negroes. Southerners see them all the time. Northerners never think about them whereas Southerners are never really thinking of anything else. Negroes are, therefore, ignored in the North and are under surveillance in the South, and suffer hideously in both places. Neither the Southerner nor the

Northerner is able to look on the Negro simply as a man. It seems to be indispensable to the national self-esteem that the Negro be considered either as a kind of ward (in which case we are told how many Negroes, comparatively, bought Cadillacs last year and how few, comparatively, were lynched), or as a victim (in which case we are promised that he will never vote in our assemblies or go to school with our kids). They are two sides of the same coin and the South will not change—*cannot* change—until the North changes. The country will not change until it re-examines itself and discovers what it really means by freedom. In the meantime, generations keep being born, bitterness is increased by incompetence, pride, and folly, and the world shrinks around us.

It is a terrible, an inexorable, law that one cannot deny the humanity of another without diminishing one's own: in the face of one's victim, one sees oneself. Walk through the streets of Harlem and see what we, this nation, have become.

SONNY'S BLUES

I read about it in the paper, in the subway, on my way to work. I read it, and I couldn't believe it, and I read it again. Then perhaps I just stared at it, at the newsprint spelling out his name, spelling out the story. I stared at it in the swinging lights of the subway car, and in the faces and bodies of the people, and in my own face, trapped in the darkness which roared outside.

It was not to be believed and I kept telling myself that, as I walked from the subway station to the high school. And at the same time I couldn't doubt it. I was scared, scared for Sonny. He became real to me again. A great block of ice got settled in my belly and kept melting there slowly all day long, while I taught my classes algebra. It was a special kind of ice. It kept melting, sending trickles of ice water all up and down my veins, but it never got less. Sometimes it hardened and seemed to expand until I felt my guts were going to come spilling out or that I was going to choke or scream. This would always be at a moment when I was remembering some specific thing Sonny had once said or done.

When he was about as old as the boys in my classes his face had been bright and open, there was a lot of copper in it; and he'd had wonderfully direct brown eyes, and great gentleness and privacy. I wondered what he looked like now. He had been picked up, the evening before, in a raid on an apartment downtown, for peddling and using heroin.

I couldn't believe it: but what I mean by that is that I couldn't find any room for it anywhere inside me. I had kept it outside me for a long time. I hadn't wanted to know. I had had suspicions, but I didn't name them, I kept putting them away. I told myself that Sonny was wild, but he wasn't crazy. And he'd always been a good boy, he hadn't ever turned hard or evil or disrespectful, the way kids can, so quick, so quick, especially in Harlem. I didn't want to believe that I'd ever see my brother going down, coming to nothing, all that light in his face gone out, in the condition I'd already seen so many others. Yet it had happened and here I was, talking about algebra to a lot of boys who might, every one of them for all I knew, be popping off needles every time they went to the head. Maybe it did more for them than algebra could.

I was sure that the first time Sonny had ever had horse, he couldn't have been much older than these boys were now. These boys, now, were living as we'd been living then, they were growing up with a rush and their heads bumped abruptly against the low ceiling of their actual possibilities. They were filled with rage. All they really knew were two darknesses, the darkness of their lives, which was now closing in on them, and the darkness of the movies, which had blinded them to that other darkness, and in which they now, vindictively, dreamed, at once more together than they were at any other time, and more alone.

When the last bell rang, the last class ended, I let out my breath. It seemed I'd been holding it for all that time. My clothes were wet—I may have looked as though I'd been sitting in a steam bath, all dressed up, all afternoon. I sat alone in the classroom a long time. I listened to the boys outside, downstairs, shouting and cursing and laughing. Their laughter struck me for perhaps the first time. It was not the joyous laughter which—God knows why—one associates with children. It was mocking and insular, its intent was to denigrate. It was disenchanted, and in this, also, lay the authority of their curses. Perhaps I was listening to them because I was thinking about my brother and in them I heard my brother. And myself.

One boy was whistling a tune, at once very complicated and very simple, it seemed to be pouring out of him as though he were a bird, and it sounded very cool and moving through all that harsh, bright air, only just holding its own through all those other sounds.

I stood up and walked over to the window and looked down into the courtyard. It was the beginning of the spring and the sap was rising in the boys. A teacher passed through them every now and again, quickly, as though he or she couldn't wait to get out of that courtyard, to get those boys out of their sight and off their minds. I started collecting my stuff. I thought I'd better get home and talk to Isabel.

The courtyard was almost deserted by the time I got downstairs. I saw this boy standing in the shadow of a doorway, looking just like Sonny. I almost called his name. Then I saw that it wasn't Sonny, but somebody we used to know, a boy from around our block. He'd been Sonny's friend. He'd never been mine, having been too young for me, and, anyway, I'd never liked him. And now, even though he was a grown-up man, he still hung around that block, still spent hours on the street corners, was always high and raggy. I used to run into him from time to time and he'd often work around to asking me for a quarter or fifty cents. He always had some real good excuse, too, and I always gave it to him, I don't know why.

But now, abruptly, I hated him. I couldn't stand the way he looked at me, partly like a dog, partly like a cunning child. I wanted to ask him what the hell he was doing in the school courtyard.

He sort of shuffled over to me, and he said, "I see you got the papers. So you already know about it."

"You mean about Sonny? Yes, I already know about it. How come they didn't get you?"

He grinned. It made him repulsive and it also brought to mind what he'd looked like as a kid. "I wasn't there. I stay away from them people."

"Good for you." I offered him a cigarette and I watched him through the smoke. "You come all the way down here just to tell me about Sonny?"

"That's right." He was sort of shaking his head and his eyes looked strange, as though they were about to cross. The bright sun deadened his damp dark brown skin and it made his eyes look yellow and showed up the dirt in his kinked hair. He smelled funky. I moved a little away from him and I said, "Well, thanks. But I already know about it and I got to get home."

"I'll walk you a little ways," he said. We started walking. There were a couple of kids still loitering in the courtyard and one of them said goodnight to me and looked strangely at the boy beside me.

"What're you going to do?" he asked me. "I mean, about Sonny?"

"Look. I haven't seen Sonny for over a year, I'm not sure I'm going to do anything. Anyway, what the hell *can* I do?"

"That's right," he said quickly, "ain't nothing you can do. Can't much help old Sonny no more, I guess."

It was what I was thinking and so it seemed to me he had no right to say it.

"I'm surprised at Sonny, though," he went on—he had a funny way of talking, he looked straight ahead as though he were talking to himself—"I thought Sonny was a smart boy, I thought he was too smart to get hung."

"I guess he thought so too," I said sharply, "and that's how he got hung. And how about you? You're pretty goddamn smart, I bet."

Then he looked directly at me, just for a minute. "I ain't smart," he said. "If I was smart, I'd have reached for a pistol a long time ago."

"Look. Don't tell *me* your sad story, if it was up to me, I'd give you one." Then I felt guilty—guilty, probably, for never having supposed that the poor bastard *had* a story of his own, much less a sad one, and I asked, quickly, "What's going to happen to him now?"

He didn't answer this. He was off by himself some place. "Funny thing," he said, and from his tone we might have been discussing the quickest way to get to Brooklyn, "when I saw the papers this morning, the first thing I asked myself was if I had anything to do with it. I felt sort of responsible."

I began to listen more carefully. The subway station was on the corner, just before us, and I stopped. He stopped, too. We were in front of a bar and he ducked slightly, peering in, but whoever he was looking for didn't seem to be there. The juke box was blasting away with something black and bouncy and I half watched the barmaid as she danced her way from the juke box to her place behind the bar. And I watched her face as she laughingly responded to something someone said to her, still keeping time to the music. When she smiled one saw the little girl, one sensed the doomed, still-struggling woman beneath the battered face of the semi-whore.

"I never *give* Sonny nothing," the boy said finally, "but a long time ago I come to school high and Sonny asked me how it felt." He paused, I couldn't bear to watch him, I watched the barmaid, and I listened to the music which seemed to be causing the pavement to shake. "I told him it felt great." The music stopped, the barmaid paused and watched the juke box until the music began again. "It did."

All this was carrying me some place I didn't want to go. I certainly didn't want to know how it felt. It filled everything, the people, the houses, the music, the dark, quicksilver barmaid, with menace; and this menace was their reality.

"What's going to happen to him now?" I asked again.

"They'll send him away some place and they'll try to cure him." He shook his head. "Maybe he'll even think he's kicked the habit. Then they'll let him loose"—he gestured, throwing his cigarette into the gutter. "That's all."

"What do you mean, that's *all*?"

But I knew what he meant.

"I *mean, that's all.*" He turned his head and looked at me, pulling down the corners of his mouth. "Don't you know what I mean?" he asked, softly.

"How the hell *would* I know what you mean?" I almost whispered it, I don't know why.

"That's right," he said to the air, "how would *he* know what I mean?" He turned toward me again, patient and calm, and yet I somehow felt him shaking, shaking as though he were going to fall apart. I felt that ice in my guts again, the dread I'd felt all afternoon; and again I watched the barmaid, moving about the bar, washing glasses, and singing. "Listen. They'll let him out and then it'll just start all over again. That's what I mean."

"You mean—they'll let him out. And then he'll just start working his way back in again. You mean he'll never kick the habit. Is that what you mean?"

"That's right," he said, cheerfully. "*You* see what I mean."

"Tell me," I said at last, "why does he want to die? He must want to die, he's killing himself, why does he want to die?"

He looked at me in surprise. He licked his lips. "He don't want to die. He wants to live. Don't nobody want to die, ever."

Then I wanted to ask him—too many things. He could not have answered, or if he had, I could not have borne the answers. I started walking. "Well, I guess it's none of my business."

"It's going to be rough on old Sonny," he said. We reached the subway station. "This is your station?" he asked. I nodded. I took one step down. "Damn!" he said, suddenly. I looked up at him. He grinned again. "Damn it if I didn't leave all my money home. You ain't got a dollar on you, have you? Just for a couple of days, is all."

All at once something inside gave and threatened to come pouring out of me. I didn't hate him any more. I felt that in another moment I'd start crying like a child.

"Sure," I said. "Don't sweat." I looked in my wallet and didn't have a dollar, I only had a five. "Here," I said. "That hold you?"

He didn't look at it—he didn't want to look at it. A terrible, closed look came over his face, as though he were keeping the number on the bill a secret from him and me. "Thanks," he said, and now he was dying to see me go. "Don't worry about Sonny. Maybe I'll write him or something."

"Sure," I said. "You do that. So long."

"Be seeing you," he said. I went on down the steps.

And I didn't write Sonny or send him anything for a long time. When I finally did, it was just after my little girl died, he wrote me back a letter which made me feel like a bastard.

Here's what he said:

Dear brother,

You don't know how much I needed to hear from you. I wanted to write you many a time but I dug how much I must have hurt you and so I didn't write. But now I feel like a man who's been trying to climb up out of some deep, real deep and funky hole and just saw the sun up there, outside. I got to get outside.

I can't tell you much about how I got here. I mean I don't know how to tell you. I guess I was afraid of something or I was trying to escape from something and you know I have never been very strong in the head (smile). I'm glad Mama and Daddy are dead and can't see what's happened to their son and I swear if I'd known what I was doing I would never have hurt you so, you and a lot of other fine people who were nice to me and who believed in me.

I don't want you to think it had anything to do with me being a musician. It's more than that. Or maybe less than that. I can't get anything straight in my head down here and I try not to think about what's going to happen to me when I get outside again. Sometime I think I'm going to flip and *never* get outside and sometime I think I'll come straight back. I tell you one thing, though, I'd rather blow my brains out than go through this again. But that's what they all say, so they tell me. If I tell you when I'm coming to New York and if you could meet me, I sure would appreciate it. Give my love to Isabel and the kids and I was sure sorry to hear about little Gracie. I wish I could be like Mama and say the Lord's will be done, but I don't know it seems to me that trouble is the

one thing that never does get stopped and I don't know
what good it does to blame it on the Lord. But maybe it
does some good if you believe it.

Your brother,

Sonny

Then I kept in constant touch with him and I sent him
whatever I could and I went to meet him when he came
back to New York. When I saw him many things I thought
I had forgotten came flooding back to me. This was because
I had begun, finally, to wonder about Sonny, about the
life that Sonny lived inside. This life, whatever it was, had
made him older and thinner and it had deepened the distant stillness in which he had always moved. He looked
very unlike my baby brother. Yet, when he smiled, when
we shook hands, the baby brother I'd never known
looked out from the depths of his private life, like an animal waiting to be coaxed into the light.

"How you been keeping?" he asked me.

"All right. And you?"

"Just fine." He was smiling all over his face. "It's good
to see you again."

"It's good to see you."

The seven years' difference in our ages lay between us
like a chasm: I wondered if these years would ever operate
between us as a bridge. I was remembering, and it made
it hard to catch my breath, that I had been there when

he was born; and I had heard the first words he had ever spoken. When he started to walk, he walked from our mother straight to me. I caught him just before he fell when he took the first steps he ever took in this world.

"How's Isabel?"

"Just fine. She's dying to see you."

"And the boys?"

"They're fine, too. They're anxious to see their uncle."

"Oh, come on. You know they don't remember me."

"Are you kidding? Of course they remember you."

He grinned again. We got into a taxi. We had a lot to say to each other, far too much to know how to begin.

As the taxi began to move, I asked, "You still want to go to India?"

He laughed. "You still remember that. Hell, no. This place is Indian enough for me."

"It used to belong to them," I said.

And he laughed again. "They damn sure knew what they were doing when they got rid of it."

Years ago, when he was around fourteen, he'd been all hipped on the idea of going to India. He read books about people sitting on rocks, naked, in all kinds of weather, but mostly bad, naturally, and walking barefoot through hot coals and arriving at wisdom. I used to say that it sounded to me as though they were getting away from wisdom as fast as they could. I think he sort of looked down on me for that.

"Do you mind," he asked, "if we have the driver drive alongside the park? On the west side—I haven't seen the city in so long."

"Of course not," I said. I was afraid that I might sound as though I were humoring him, but I hoped he wouldn't take it that way.

So we drove along, between the green of the park and the stony, lifeless elegance of hotels and apartment buildings, toward the vivid, killing streets of our childhood. These streets hadn't changed, though housing projects jutted up out of them now like rocks in the middle of a boiling sea. Most of the houses in which we had grown up had vanished, as had the stores from which we had stolen, the basements in which we had first tried sex, the rooftops from which we had hurled tin cans and bricks. But houses exactly like the houses of our past yet dominated the landscape, boys exactly like the boys we once had been found themselves smothering in these houses, came down into the streets for light and air and found themselves encircled by disaster. Some escaped the trap, most didn't. Those who got out always left something of themselves behind, as some animals amputate a leg and leave it in the trap. It might be said, perhaps, that I had escaped, after all, I was a school teacher; or that Sonny had, he hadn't lived in Harlem for years. Yet, as the cab moved uptown through streets which seemed, with a rush, to darken with dark people, and as I covertly studied Sonny's face, it came to me that what we both were seeking through our separate cab windows was that part of ourselves which had been left behind. It's always at the hour of trouble and confrontation that the missing member aches.

We hit 110th Street and started rolling up Lenox Avenue. And I'd known this avenue all my life, but it seemed to me again, as it had seemed on the day I'd first heard about Sonny's trouble, filled with a hidden menace which was its very breath of life.

"We almost there," said Sonny.

"Almost." We were both too nervous to say anything more.

We live in a housing project. It hasn't been up long. A few days after it was up it seemed uninhabitably new, now, of course, it's already rundown. It looks like a parody of the good, clean, faceless life—God knows the people who live in it do their best to make it a parody. The beat-looking grass lying around isn't enough to make their lives green, the hedges will never hold out the streets, and they know it. The big windows fool no one, they aren't big enough to make space out of no space. They don't bother with the windows, they watch the TV screen instead. The playground is most popular with the children who don't play at jacks, or skip rope, or roller skate, or swing, and they can be found in it after dark. We moved in partly because it's not too far from where I teach, and partly for the kids; but it's really just like the houses in which Sonny and I grew up. The same things happen, they'll have the same things to remember. The moment Sonny and I started into the house I had the feeling that I was simply bringing him back into the danger he had almost died trying to escape.

Sonny has never been talkative. So I don't know why I was sure he'd be dying to talk to me when supper was over the first night. Everything went fine, the oldest boy remembered him, and the youngest boy liked him, and Sonny had remembered to bring something for each of them; and Isabel, who is really much nicer than I am, more open and giving, had gone to a lot of trouble about dinner and was genuinely glad to see him. And she's always been able to tease Sonny in a way that I haven't. It was nice to see her face so vivid again and to hear her laugh and watch her make Sonny laugh. She wasn't, or, anyway, she didn't seem to be, at all uneasy or embarrassed. She chatted as though there were no subject which had to be avoided and she got Sonny past his first, faint stiffness. And thank God she was there, for I was filled with that icy dread again. Everything I did seemed awkward to me, and everything I said sounded freighted with hidden meaning. I was trying to remember everything I'd heard about dope addiction and I couldn't help watching Sonny for signs. I wasn't doing it out of malice. I was trying to find out something about my brother. I was dying to hear him tell me he was safe.

"Safe!" my father grunted, whenever Mama suggested trying to move to a neighborhood which might be safer for children. "Safe, hell! Ain't no place safe for kids, nor nobody."

He always went on like this, but he wasn't, ever, really as bad as he sounded, not even on weekends, when he got drunk. As a matter of fact, he was always on the lookout for "something a little better," but he died before he found it. He died suddenly, during a drunken weekend in the middle of the war, when Sonny was fifteen. He and Sonny hadn't ever got on too well. And this was partly because Sonny was the apple of his father's eye. It was because he loved Sonny so much and was frightened for him, that he was always fighting with him. It doesn't do any good to fight with Sonny. Sonny just moves back, inside himself, where he can't be reached. But the principal reason that they never hit it off is that they were so much alike. Daddy was big and rough and loud-talking, just the opposite of Sonny, but they both had—that same privacy.

Mama tried to tell me something about this, just after Daddy died. I was home on leave from the army.

This was the last time I ever saw my mother alive. Just the same, this picture gets all mixed up in my mind with pictures I had of her when she was younger. The way I always see her is the way she used to be on a Sunday afternoon, say, when the old folks were talking after the big Sunday dinner. I always see her wearing pale blue. She'd be sitting on the sofa. And my father would be sitting in the easy chair, not far from her. And the living room would be full of church folks and relatives. There they sit, in chairs all around the living room, and the night is creeping up outside, but nobody knows it yet. You can see the darkness growing against the windowpanes and you hear the street noises every now and again, or maybe the jangling beat of a tambourine from one of the churches close by, but it's real quiet in the room. For a moment nobody's talking, but every face looks darkening, like the sky outside. And my mother rocks a little from the waist, and my father's eyes are closed. Everyone is looking at something a child can't see. For a minute they've forgotten the children. Maybe a kid is lying on the rug, half asleep. Maybe somebody's got a kid in his lap and is absent-mindedly stroking the kid's head. Maybe there's a kid, quiet and big-eyed, curled up in a big chair in the corner. The silence, the darkness coming, and the darkness in the faces frightens the child obscurely. He hopes that the hand which strokes his forehead will never stop— will never die. He hopes that there will never come a time when the old folks won't be sitting around the living room, talking about where they've come from, and what they've seen, and what's happened to them and their kinfolk.

But something deep and watchful in the child knows that this is bound to end, is already ending. In a moment someone will get up and turn on the light. Then the old folks will remember the children and they won't talk any more that day. And when light fills the room, the child is filled with darkness. He knows that every time this happens he's moved just a little closer to that darkness outside. The darkness outside is what the old folks have been talking about. It's what they've come from. It's what they endure. The child knows that they won't talk any more because if he knows too much about what's happened to *them,* he'll know too much too soon, about what's going to happen to *him.*

The last time I talked to my mother, I remember I was restless. I wanted to get out and see Isabel. We weren't married then and we had a lot to straighten out between us.

There Mama sat, in black, by the window. She was humming an old church song, *Lord, you brought me from a long ways off.* Sonny was out somewhere. Mama kept watching the streets.

"I don't know," she said, "if I'll ever see you again, after you go off from here. But I hope you'll remember the things I tried to teach you."

"Don't talk like that," I said, and smiled. "You'll be here a long time yet."

She smiled, too, but she said nothing. She was quiet for

a long time. And I said, "Mama, don't you worry about nothing. I'll be writing all the time, and you be getting the checks. . . ."

"I want to talk to you about your brother," she said, suddenly. "If anything happens to me he ain't going to have nobody to look out for him."

"Mama," I said, "ain't nothing going to happen to you *or* Sonny. Sonny's all right. He's a good boy and he's got good sense."

"It ain't a question of his being a good boy," Mama said, "nor of his having good sense. It ain't only the bad ones, nor yet the dumb ones that gets sucked under." She stopped, looking at me. "Your Daddy once had a brother," she said, and she smiled in a way that made me feel she was in pain. "You didn't never know that, did you?"

"No," I said, "I never knew that," and I watched her face.

"Oh, yes," she said, "your Daddy had a brother." She looked out of the window again. "I know you never saw your Daddy cry. But *I* did—many a time, through all these years."

I asked her, "What happened to his brother? How come nobody's ever talked about him?"

This was the first time I ever saw my mother look old.

"His brother got killed," she said, "when he was just a little younger than you are now. I knew him. He was a fine boy. He was maybe a little full of the devil, but he didn't mean nobody no harm."

Then she stopped and the room was silent, exactly as it had sometimes been on those Sunday afternoons. Mama kept looking out into the streets.

"He used to have a job in the mill," she said, "and, like all young folks, he just liked to perform on Saturday nights. Saturday nights, him and your father would drift around to different place, go to dances and things like that, or just sit around with people they knew, and your father's brother would sing, he had a fine voice, and play along with himself on his guitar. Well, this particular Saturday night, him and your father was coming home from some place, and they were both a little drunk and there was a moon that night, it was bright like day. Your father's brother was feeling kind of good, and he was whistling to himself, and he had his guitar slung over his shoulder. They was coming down a hill and beneath them was a road that turned off from the highway. Well, your father's brother, being always kind of frisky, decided to run down this hill, and he did, with that guitar banging and clanging behind him, and he ran across the road, and he was making water behind a tree. And your father was sort of amused at him and he was still coming down the hill, kind of slow. Then he heard a car motor and that same minute his brother stepped from behind the tree, into the road, in the moonlight. And he started to cross the road. And your father started to run down the hill, he says he don't know why. This car was full of white men. They was all drunk, and when they seen your father's brother they let out a great whoop and holler and they aimed the car straight at him. They was having fun, they just wanted to scare him, the way they do sometimes, you know. But they was drunk. And I guess the boy, being drunk, too, and scared, kind of lost his head. By the time he jumped it was too late. Your father says he heard his brother scream when the car rolled over him, and he heard the wood of that guitar when it give, and he heard them strings go flying, and he heard them white men shouting, and the car kept on a-going and it ain't stopped till this day. And, time your father got down the hill, his brother weren't nothing but blood and pulp."

Tears were gleaming on my mother's face. There wasn't anything I could say.

"He never mentioned it," she said, "because I never let him mention it before you children. Your Daddy was like a crazy man that night and for many a night thereafter. He says he never in his life seen anything as dark as that road after the lights of that car had gone away. Weren't nothing, weren't nobody on that road, just your Daddy and his brother and that busted guitar. Oh, yes. Your Daddy never did really get right again. Till the day he died he weren't sure but that every white man he saw was the man that killed his brother."

She stopped and took out her handkerchief and dried her eyes and looked at me.

"I ain't telling you all this," she said, "to make you scared or bitter or to make you hate nobody. I'm telling you this because you got a brother. And the world ain't changed."

I guess I didn't want to believe this. I guess she saw this in my face. She turned away from me, toward the window again, searching those streets.

"But I praise my Redeemer," she said at last, "that He called your Daddy home before me. I ain't saying it to throw no flowers at myself, but, I declare, it keeps me from feeling too cast down to know I helped your father get safely through this world. Your father always acted like he was the roughest, strongest man on earth. And everybody took him to be like that. But if he hadn't had *me* there—to see his tears!"

She was crying again. Still, I couldn't move. I said, "Lord, Lord, Mama, I didn't know it was like that."

"Oh, honey," she said, "there's a lot that you don't know. But you are going to find it out." She stood up from the window and came over to me. "You got to hold on to your brother," she said, "and don't let him fall, no matter what it looks like is happening to him and no matter how evil you gets with him. You going to be evil with him many a time. But don't you forget what I told you, you hear?"

"I won't forget," I said. "Don't you worry, I won't forget. I won't let nothing happen to Sonny."

My mother smiled as though she were amused at something she saw in my face. Then, "You may not be able to stop nothing from happening. But you got to let him know you's *there*."

Two days later I was married, and then I was gone. And I had a lot of things on my mind and I pretty well forgot my promise to Mama until I got shipped home on a special furlough for her funeral.

And, after the funeral, with just Sonny and me alone in the empty kitchen, I tried to find out something about him.

"What do you want to do?" I asked him.

"I'm going to be a musician," he said.

For he had graduated, in the time I had been away, from dancing to the juke box to finding out who was playing what, and what they were doing with it, and he had bought himself a set of drums.

"You mean, you want to be a drummer?" I somehow had the feeling that being a drummer might be all right for other people but not for my brother Sonny.

"I don't think," he said, looking at me very gravely, "that I'll ever be a good drummer. But I think I can play a piano."

I frowned. I'd never played the role of the older brother quite so seriously before, had scarcely ever, in fact, *asked* Sonny a damn thing. I sensed myself in the presence of something I didn't really know how to handle, didn't understand. So I made my frown a little deeper as I asked: "What kind of musician do you want to be?"

He grinned. "How many kinds do you think there are?"

"Be *serious*," I said.

He laughed, throwing his head back, and then looked at me. "I *am* serious."

"Well, then, for Christ's sake, stop kidding around and answer a serious question. I mean, do you want to be a concert pianist, you want to play classical music and all that, or—or what?" Long before I finished he was laughing again. "For Christ's *sake*, Sonny!"

He sobered, but with difficulty. "I'm sorry. But you sound so—*scared*!" and he was off again.

"Well, you may think it's funny now, baby, but it's not going to be so funny when you have to make your living at it, let me tell you *that*." I was furious because I knew he was laughing at me and I didn't know why.

"No," he said, very sober now, and afraid, perhaps, that he'd hurt me, "I don't want to be a classical pianist. That isn't what interests me. I mean"—he paused, looking hard at me, as though his eyes would help me to understand, and then gestured helplessly, as though perhaps his hand would help—"I mean, I'll have a lot of studying to do, and I'll have to study *everything,* but, I mean, I want to play *with*—jazz musicians." He stopped. "I want to play jazz," he said.

Well, the word had never before sounded as heavy, as real, as it sounded that afternoon in Sonny's mouth. I just looked at him and I was probably frowning a real frown by this time. I simply couldn't see why on earth he'd want to spend his time hanging around nightclubs, clowning around on bandstands, while people pushed each other around a dance floor. It seemed—beneath him, somehow. I had never thought about it before, had never been forced to, but I suppose I had always put jazz musicians in a class with what Daddy called "good-time people."

"Are you *serious*?"

"Hell, *yes,* I'm serious."

He looked more helpless than ever, and annoyed, and deeply hurt.

I suggested, helpfully: "You mean—like Louis Armstrong?"

His face closed as though I'd struck him. "No. I'm not talking about none of that old-time, down home crap."

"Well, look, Sonny, I'm sorry, don't get mad. I just don't altogether get it, that's all. Name somebody—you know, a jazz musician you admire."

"Bird."

"Who?"

"Bird! Charlie Parker! Don't they teach you nothing in the goddamn army?"

I lit a cigarette. I was surprised and then a little amused to discover that I was trembling. "I've been out of touch," I said. "You'll have to be patient with me. Now. Who's this Parker character?"

"He's just one of the greatest jazz musicians alive," said Sonny, sullenly, his hands in his pockets, his back to me. "Maybe *the* greatest," he added, bitterly, "that's probably why *you* never heard of him."

"All right," I said, "I'm ignorant. I'm sorry. I'll go out and buy all the cat's records right away, all right?"

"It don't," said Sonny, with dignity, "make any difference to me. I don't care what you listen to. Don't do me no favors."

I was beginning to realize that I'd never seen him so upset before. With another part of my mind I was thinking that this would probably turn out to be one of those things kids go through and that I shouldn't make it seem important by pushing it too hard. Still, I didn't think it would do any harm to ask: "Doesn't all this take a lot of time? Can you make a living at it?"

He turned back to me and half leaned, half sat, on the kitchen table. "Everything takes time," he said, "and— well, yes, sure, I can make a living at it. But what I don't seem to be able to make you understand is that it's the only thing I want to do."

"Well, Sonny," I said, gently, "you know people can't always do exactly what they *want* to do—"

"*No,* I don't know that," said Sonny, surprising me. "I think people *ought* to do what they want to do, what else are they alive for?"

"You getting to be a big boy," I said desperately, "it's time you started thinking about your future."

"I'm thinking about my future," said Sonny, grimly. "I think about it all the time."

I gave up. I decided, if he didn't change his mind, that we could always talk about it later. "In the meantime," I said, "you got to finish school." We had already decided that he'd have to move in with Isabel and her folks. I knew this wasn't the ideal arrangement because Isabel's folks are inclined to be dicty and they hadn't especially wanted Isabel to marry me. But I didn't know what else to do. "And we have to get you fixed up at Isabel's."

There was a long silence. He moved from the kitchen table to the window. "That's a terrible idea. You know it yourself."

"Do you have a *better* idea?"

He just walked up and down the kitchen for a minute. He was as tall as I was. He had started to shave. I suddenly had the feeling that I didn't know him at all.

He stopped at the kitchen table and picked up my cig-arettes. Looking at me with a kind of mocking, amused defiance, he put one between his lips. "You mind?"

"You smoking already?"

He lit the cigarette and nodded, watching me through

the smoke. "I just wanted to see if I'd have the courage to smoke in front of you." He grinned and blew a great cloud of smoke to the ceiling. "It was easy." He looked at my face. "Come on, now. I bet you was smoking at my age, tell the truth."

I didn't say anything but the truth was on my face, and he laughed. But now there was something very strained in his laugh. "Sure. And I bet that ain't all you was doing."

He was frightening me a little. "Cut the crap," I said. "We already decided that you was going to go and live at Isabel's. Now what's got into you all of a sudden?"

"*You* decided it," he pointed out. "*I* didn't decide nothing." He stopped in front of me, leaning against the stove, arms loosely folded. "Look, brother. I don't want to stay in Harlem no more, I really don't." He was very earnest. He looked at me, then over toward the kitchen window. There was something in his eyes I'd never seen before, some thoughtfulness, some worry all his own. He rubbed the muscle of one arm. "It's time I was getting out of here."

"Where do you want to *go,* Sonny?"

"I want to join the army. Or the navy, I don't care. If I say I'm old enough, they'll believe me."

Then I got mad. It was because I was so scared. "You must be crazy. You goddamn fool, what the hell do you want to go and join the *army* for?"

"I just told you. To get out of Harlem."

"Sonny, you haven't even finished *school.* And if you

really want to be a musician, how do you expect to study if you're in the *army*?"

He looked at me, trapped, and in anguish. "There's ways. I might be able to work out some kind of deal. Anyway, I'll have the G.I. Bill when I come out."

"*If* you come out." We stared at each other. "Sonny, please. Be reasonable. I know the setup is far from perfect. But we got to do the best we can."

"I ain't learning nothing in school," he said. "Even when I go." He turned away from me and opened the window and threw his cigarette out into the narrow alley. I watched his back. "At least, I ain't learning nothing you'd want me to learn." He slammed the window so hard I thought the glass would fly out, and turned back to me. "And I'm sick of the stink of these garbage cans!"

"Sonny," I said, "I know how you feel. But if you don't finish school now, you're going to be sorry later that you didn't." I grabbed him by the shoulders. "And you only got another year. It ain't so bad. And I'll come back and I swear I'll help you do *whatever* you want to do. Just try to put up with it till I come back. Will you please do that? For me?"

He didn't answer and he wouldn't look at me.

"Sonny. You hear me?"

He pulled away. "I hear you. But you never hear anything *I* say."

I didn't know what to say to that. He looked out of the

window and then back at me. "OK," he said, and sighed. "I'll try."

Then I said, trying to cheer him up a little, "They got a piano at Isabel's. You can practice on it."

And as a matter of fact, it did cheer him up for a minute. "That's right," he said to himself. "I forgot that." His face relaxed a little. But the worry, the thoughtfulness, played on it still, the way shadows play on a face which is staring into the fire.

But I thought I'd never hear the end of that piano. At first, Isabel would write me, saying how nice it was that Sonny was so serious about his music and how, as soon as he came in from school, or wherever he had been when he was supposed to be at school, he went straight to that piano and stayed there until suppertime. And, after supper, he went back to that piano and stayed there until everybody went to bed. He was at the piano all day Saturday and all day Sunday. Then he bought a record player and started playing records. He'd play one record over and over again, all day long sometimes, and he'd improvise along with it on the piano. Or he'd play one section of the record, one chord, one change, one progression, then he'd do it on the piano. Then back to the record. Then back to the piano.

Well, I really don't know how they stood it. Isabel finally confessed that it wasn't like living with a person at all, it was like living with sound. And the sound didn't make any sense to her, didn't make any sense to any of them—naturally. They began, in a way, to be afflicted by this presence that was living in their home. It was as though Sonny were some sort of god, or monster. He moved in an atmosphere which wasn't like theirs at all. They fed him and he ate, he washed himself, he walked in and out of their door; he certainly wasn't nasty or unpleasant or rude, Sonny isn't any of those things; but it was as though he were all wrapped up in some cloud, some fire, some vision all his own; and there wasn't any way to reach him.

At the same time, he wasn't really a man yet, he was still a child, and they had to watch out for him in all kinds of ways. They certainly couldn't throw him out. Neither did they dare to make a great scene about that piano because even they dimly sensed, as I sensed, from so many thousands of miles away, that Sonny was at that piano playing for his life.

But he hadn't been going to school. One day a letter came from the school board and Isabel's mother got it— there had, apparently, been other letters but Sonny had torn them up. This day, when Sonny came in, Isabel's mother showed him the letter and asked where he'd been spending his time. And she finally got it out of him that he'd been down in Greenwich Village, with musicians and other characters, in a white girl's apartment. And this scared her and she started to scream at him and what came up, once she began—though she denies it to this day—was what sacrifices they were making to give Sonny a decent home and how little he appreciated it.

Sonny didn't play the piano that day. By evening, Isabel's mother had calmed down but then there was the old man to deal with, and Isabel herself. Isabel says she did her best to be calm but she broke down and started crying. She says she just watched Sonny's face. She could tell, by watching him, what was happening with him. And what was happening was that they penetrated his cloud, they had reached him. Even if their fingers had been a thousand times more gentle than human fingers ever are, he could hardly help feeling that they had stripped him naked and were spitting on that nakedness. For he also had to see that his presence, that music, which was life or death to him, had been torture for them and that they had endured it, not at all for his sake, but only for mine. And Sonny couldn't take that. He can take it a little better today than he could then but he's still not very good at it and, frankly, I don't know anybody who is.

The silence of the next few days must have been louder than the sound of all the music ever played since time began. One morning, before she went to work, Isabel was in his room for something and she suddenly realized that all of his records were gone. And she knew for certain that he was gone. And he was. He went as far as the navy would carry him. He finally sent me a postcard from some place in Greece and that was the first I knew that Sonny was still alive. I didn't see him any more until we were both back in New York and the war had long been over.

He was a man by then, of course, but I wasn't willing to see it. He came by the house from time to time, but we fought almost every time we met. I didn't like the way he carried himself, loose and dreamlike all the time, and I didn't like his friends, and his music seemed to be merely an excuse for the life he led. It sounded just that weird and disordered.

Then we had a fight, a pretty awful fight, and I didn't see him for months. By and by I looked him up, where he was living, in a furnished room in the Village, and I tried to make it up. But there were lots of other people in the room and Sonny just lay on his bed, and he wouldn't come downstairs with me, and he treated these other people as though they were his family and I weren't. So I got mad and then he got mad, and then I told him that he might just as well be dead as live the way he was living. Then he stood up and he told me not to worry about him any more in life, that he *was* dead as far as I was concerned. Then he pushed me to the door and the other people looked on as though nothing were happening, and he slammed the door behind me. I stood in the hallway, staring at the door. I heard somebody laugh in the room and then the tears came to my eyes. I started down the steps, whistling to keep from crying, I kept whistling to myself, *You going to need me, baby, one of these cold, rainy days.*

I read about Sonny's trouble in the spring. Little Grace died in the fall. She was a beautiful little girl. But she only lived a little over two years. She died of polio and she suffered. She had a slight fever for a couple of days, but it didn't seem like anything and we just kept her in bed. And we would certainly have called the doctor, but the fever dropped, she seemed to be all right. So we thought it had just been a cold. Then, one day, she was up, playing, Isabel was in the kitchen fixing lunch for the two boys when they'd come in from school, and she heard Grace fall down in the living room. When you have a lot of children you don't always start running when one of them falls, unless they start screaming or something. And, this time, Grace was quiet. Yet, Isabel says that when she heard that *thump* and then that silence, something happened in her to make her afraid. And she ran to the living room and there was little Grace on the floor, all twisted up, and the reason she hadn't screamed was that she couldn't get her breath. And when she did scream, it was the worst sound, Isabel says, that she'd ever heard in all her life, and she still hears it sometimes in her dreams. Isabel will sometimes wake me up with a low, moaning, strangled sound and I have to be quick to awaken her and hold her to me and where Isabel is weeping against me seems a mortal wound.

I think I may have written Sonny the very day that little Grace was buried. I was sitting in the living room in the dark, by myself, and I suddenly thought of Sonny. My trouble made his real.

One Saturday afternoon, when Sonny had been living with us, or, anyway, been in our house, for nearly two weeks, I found myself wandering aimlessly about the living room, drinking from a can of beer, and trying to work up the courage to search Sonny's room. He was out, he was usually out whenever I was home, and Isabel had taken the children to see their grandparents. Suddenly I was standing still in front of the living room window, watching Seventh Avenue. The idea of searching Sonny's room made me still. I scarcely dared to admit to myself what I'd be searching for. I didn't know what I'd do if I found it. Or if I didn't.

On the sidewalk across from me, near the entrance to a barbecue joint, some people were holding an old-fashioned revival meeting. The barbecue cook, wearing a dirty white apron, his conked hair reddish and metallic in the pale sun, and a cigarette between his lips, stood in the doorway, watching them. Kids and older people paused in their errands and stood there, along with some older men and a couple of very tough-looking women who watched everything that happened on the avenue, as though they owned it, or were maybe owned by it. Well, they were watching this, too. The revival was being carried on by three sisters in black, and a brother. All they had were their voices and their Bibles and a tambourine. The brother was testifying and while he testified two of the sisters stood together, seeming to say, amen, and the third sister walked around with the tambourine outstretched and a couple of people dropped coins into it. Then the brother's testimony ended and the sister who had been taking up the collection dumped the coins into her palm and transferred them to the pocket of her long black robe. Then she raised both hands, striking the tambourine against the air, and then against one hand, and she started to sing. And the two other sisters and the brother joined in.

It was strange, suddenly, to watch, though I had been seeing these street meetings all my life. So, of course, had everybody else down there. Yet, they paused and watched and listened and I stood still at the window. *"Tis the old ship of Zion,"* they sang, and the sister with the tambourine kept a steady, jangling beat, *"it has rescued many a thousand!"* Not a soul under the sound of their voices was hearing this song for the first time, not one of them had been rescued. Nor had they seen much in the way of rescue work being done around them. Neither did they especially believe in the holiness of the three sisters and the brother, they knew too much about them, knew where they lived, and how. The woman with the tam-

bourine, whose voice dominated the air, whose face was
bright with joy, was divided by very little from the woman
who stood watching her, a cigarette between her heavy,
chapped lips, her hair a cuckoo's nest, her face scarred and
swollen from many beatings, and her black eyes glittering
like coal. Perhaps they both knew this, which was why,
when, as rarely, they addressed each other, they addressed
each other as Sister. As the singing filled the air the watching, listening faces underwent a change, the eyes focusing
on something within; the music seemed to soothe a poison
out of them; and time seemed, nearly, to fall away from the
sullen, belligerent, battered faces, as though they were fleeing back to their first condition, while dreaming of their
last. The barbecue cook half shook his head and smiled,
and dropped his cigarette and disappeared into his joint. A
man fumbled in his pockets for change and stood holding
it in his hand impatiently, as though he had just remembered a pressing appointment further up the avenue. He
looked furious. Then I saw Sonny, standing on the edge of
the crowd. He was carrying a wide, flat notebook with a
green cover, and it made him look, from where I was standing, almost like a schoolboy. The coppery sun brought
out the copper in his skin, he was very faintly smiling,
standing very still. Then the singing stopped, the tambourine turned into a collection plate again. The furious
man dropped in his coins and vanished, so did a couple of

the women, and Sonny dropped some change in the plate, looking directly at the woman with a little smile. He started across the avenue, toward the house. He has a slow, loping walk, something like the way Harlem hipsters walk, only he's imposed on this his own half-beat. I had never really noticed it before.

I stayed at the window, both relieved and apprehensive. As Sonny disappeared from my sight, they began singing again. And they were still singing when his key turned in the lock.

"Hey," he said.

"Hey, yourself. You want some beer?"

"No. Well, maybe." But he came up to the window and stood beside me, looking out. "What a warm voice," he said.

They were singing *If I could only hear my mother pray again!*

"Yes," I said, "and she can sure beat that tambourine."

"But what a terrible song," he said, and laughed. He dropped his notebook on the sofa and disappeared into the kitchen. "Where's Isabel and the kids?"

"I think they went to see their grandparents. You hungry?"

"No." He came back into the living room with his can of beer. "You want to come some place with me tonight?"

I sensed, I don't know how, that I couldn't possibly say no. "Sure. Where?"

He sat down on the sofa and picked up his notebook and started leafing through it. "I'm going to sit in with some fellows in a joint in the Village."

"You mean, you're going to play, tonight?"

"That's right." He took a swallow of his beer and moved back to the window. He gave me a sidelong look. "If you can stand it."

"I'll try," I said.

He smiled to himself and we both watched as the meeting across the way broke up. The three sisters and the brother, heads bowed, were singing *God be with you till we meet again.* The faces around them were very quiet. Then the song ended. The small crowd dispersed. We watched the three women and the lone man walk slowly up the avenue.

"When she was singing before," said Sonny, abruptly, "her voice reminded me for a minute of what heroin feels like sometimes—when it's in your veins. It makes you feel sort of warm and cool at the same time. And distant. And—and sure." He sipped his beer, very deliberately not looking at me. I watched his face. "It makes you feel—in control. Sometimes you've got to have that feeling."

"Do you?" I sat down slowly in the easy chair.

"Sometimes." He went to the sofa and picked up his notebook again. "Some people do."

"In order," I asked, "to play?" And my voice was very ugly, full of contempt and anger.

"Well"—he looked at me with great, troubled eyes, as though, in fact, he hoped his eyes would tell me things he could never otherwise say—"they *think* so. And *if* they think so—!"

"And what do *you* think?" I asked.

He sat on the sofa and put his can of beer on the floor. "I don't know," he said, and I couldn't be sure if he were answering my question or pursuing his thoughts. His face didn't tell me. "It's not so much to *play*. It's to *stand* it, to be able to make it at all. On any level." He frowned and smiled: "In order to keep from shaking to pieces."

"But these friends of yours," I said, "they seem to shake themselves to pieces pretty goddamn fast."

"Maybe." He played with the notebook. And something told me that I should curb my tongue, that Sonny was doing his best to talk, that I should listen. "But of course you only know the ones that've gone to pieces. Some don't—or at least they haven't *yet* and that's just about all *any* of us can say." He paused. "And then there are some who just live, really, in hell, and they know it and they see what's happening and they go right on. I don't know." He sighed, dropped the notebook, folded his arms. "Some guys, you can tell from the way they play, they on something *all* the time. And you can see that, well, it makes something real for them. But of course," he picked up his beer from the floor and sipped it and put the can down again, "they *want* to, too, you've got to see that. Even some of them that say they don't—*some,* not all."

"And what about you?" I asked—I couldn't help it. "What about you? Do *you* want to?"

He stood up and walked to the window and remained silent for a long time. Then he sighed. "Me," he said. Then: "While I was downstairs before, on my way here, listening to that woman sing, it struck me all of a sudden how much suffering she must have had to go through—to sing like that. It's *repulsive* to think you have to suffer that much."

I said: "But there's no way not to suffer—is there, Sonny?"

"I believe not," he said and smiled, "but that's never stopped anyone from trying." He looked at me. "Has it?" I realized, with this mocking look, that there stood between us, forever, beyond the power of time or forgiveness, the fact that I had held silence—so long!—when he had needed human speech to help him. He turned back to the window. "No, there's no way not to suffer. But you try all kinds of ways to keep from drowning in it, to keep on top of it, and to make it seem—well, like *you.* Like you did something, all right, and now you're suffering for it. You know?" I said nothing. "Well you know," he said, impatiently, "why *do* people suffer? Maybe it's better to do something to give it a reason, *any* reason."

"But we just agreed," I said, "that there's no way not to suffer. Isn't it better, then, just to—take it?"

"But nobody just takes it," Sonny cried, "that's what I'm telling you! *Everybody* tries not to. You're just hung up on the *way* some people try—it's not *your* way!"

The hair on my face began to itch, my face felt wet. "That's not true," I said, "that's not true. I don't give a damn what other people do, I don't even care how they suffer. I just care how *you* suffer." And he looked at me. "Please believe me," I said, "I don't want to see you— die—trying not to suffer."

"I won't," he said, flatly, "die trying not to suffer. At least, not any faster than anybody else."

"But there's no need," I said, trying to laugh, "is there? in killing yourself."

I wanted to say more, but I couldn't. I wanted to talk about will power and how life could be—well, beautiful. I wanted to say that it was all within; but was it? or, rather, wasn't that exactly the trouble? And I wanted to promise that I would never fail him again. But it would all have sounded—empty words and lies.

So I made the promise to myself and prayed that I would keep it.

"It's terrible sometimes, inside," he said, "that's what's the trouble. You walk these streets, black and funky and cold, and there's not really a living ass to talk to, and there's nothing shaking, and there's no way of getting it out—that storm inside. You can't talk it and you can't make love with it, and when you finally try to get with it and play it, you realize *nobody's* listening. So *you've* got to listen. You got to find a way to listen."

And then he walked away from the window and sat on the sofa again, as though all the wind had suddenly been knocked out of him. "Sometimes you'll do *anything* to play, even cut your mother's throat." He laughed and looked at me. "Or your brother's." Then he sobered. "Or your own." Then: "Don't worry. I'm all right now and I think I'll *be* all right. But I can't forget—where I've been. I don't mean just the physical place I've been, I mean where I've *been*. And *what* I've been."

"What have you been, Sonny?" I asked.

He smiled—but sat sideways on the sofa, his elbow resting on the back, his fingers playing with his mouth and chin, not looking at me. "I've been something I didn't recognize, didn't know I could be. Didn't know anybody could be." He stopped, looking inward, looking helplessly young, looking old. "I'm not talking about it now because I feel *guilty* or anything like that—maybe it would be better if I did, I don't know. Anyway, I can't really talk about it. Not to you, not to anybody," and now he turned and faced me. "Sometimes, you know, and it was actually when I was most *out* of the world, I felt that I was in it, that I was *with* it, really; and I could play or I didn't really have to *play,* it just came out of me, it was there. And I don't know how I played, thinking about it now, but I know I did awful things, those times, sometimes, to people. Or it wasn't that I *did* anything to them—it was that they weren't real." He picked up the beer can; it was empty; he rolled it between his palms: "And other times—well, I needed a fix, I needed to find a place to lean, I needed to clear a space to *listen*—and I couldn't find it, and I—went crazy, I did terrible things to *me,* I was terrible *for* me." He began pressing the beer can between his hands, I watched the metal begin to give. It glittered, as he played with it, like a knife, and I was afraid he would cut himself, but I said nothing. "Oh well. I can never tell you. I was all by myself at the bottom of something, stinking and sweating and crying and shaking, and I smelled it, you know? *my* stink, and I thought I'd die if I couldn't get away from it and yet, all the same, I knew that everything I was doing was just locking me in with it. And I didn't know," he paused, still flattening the beer can, "I didn't know, I still *don't* know, something kept telling me that maybe it was good to smell your own stink, but I didn't think that *that* was what I'd been trying to do—and—who can stand it?" and he abruptly dropped the ruined beer can, looking at me with a small, still smile, and then rose, walking to the window as though it were the lodestone rock. I watched his face, he watched the avenue. "I couldn't tell you when Mama died—but the reason I wanted to leave Harlem so bad was to get away from drugs. And then, when I ran away, that's what I was running from—really. When I came back, nothing had changed, *I* hadn't changed, I was just—

older." And he stopped, drumming with his fingers on the windowpane. The sun had vanished, soon darkness would fall. I watched his face. "It can come again," he said, almost as though speaking to himself. Then he turned to me. "It can come again," he repeated. "I just want you to know that."

"All right," I said, at last. "So it can come again, All right."

He smiled, but the smile was sorrowful. "I had to try to tell you," he said.

"Yes," I said. "I understand that."

"You're my brother," he said, looking straight at me, and not smiling at all.

"Yes," I repeated, "yes. I understand that."

He turned back to the window, looking out. "All that hatred down there," he said, "all that hatred and misery and love. It's a wonder it doesn't blow the avenue apart."

We went to the only nightclub on a short, dark street, downtown. We squeezed through the narrow, chattering, jam-packed bar to the entrance of the big room, where the bandstand was. And we stood there for a moment, for the lights were very dim in this room and we couldn't see. Then, "Hello, boy," said a voice and an enormous black man, much older than Sonny or myself, erupted out of all that atmospheric lighting and put an arm around Sonny's shoulder. "I been sitting right here," he said, "waiting for you."

He had a big voice, too, and heads in the darkness turned toward us.

Sonny grinned and pulled a little away, and said, "Creole, this is my brother. I told you about him."

Creole shook my hand. "I'm glad to meet you, son," he said, and it was clear that he was glad to meet me *there,* for Sonny's sake. And he smiled, "You got a real musician in *your* family," and he took his arm from Sonny's shoulder and slapped him, lightly, affectionately, with the back of his hand.

"Well. Now I've heard it all," said a voice behind us. This was another musician, and a friend of Sonny's, a coal-black, cheerful-looking man, built close to the ground. He immediately began confiding to me, at the top of his lungs, the most terrible things about Sonny, his teeth gleaming like a lighthouse and his laugh coming up out of him like the beginning of an earthquake. And it turned out that everyone at the bar knew Sonny, or almost everyone; some were musicians, working there, or nearby, or not working, some were simply hangers-on, and some were there to hear Sonny play. I was introduced to all of them and they were all very polite to me. Yet, it was clear that, for them, I was only Sonny's brother. Here, I was in Sonny's world. Or, rather: his kingdom. Here, it was not even a question that his veins bore royal blood.

They were going to play soon and Creole installed me, by myself, at a table in a dark corner. Then I watched them, Creole, and the little black man, and Sonny, and the others, while they horsed around, standing just below the bandstand. The light from the bandstand spilled just a little short of them and, watching them laughing and gesturing and moving about, I had the feeling that they, nevertheless, were being most careful not to step into that circle of light too suddenly: that if they moved into the light too suddenly, without thinking, they would perish in flame. Then, while I watched, one of them, the small, black man, moved into the light and crossed the bandstand and started fooling around with his drums. Then—being funny and being, also, extremely ceremonious—Creole took Sonny by the arm and led him to the piano. A woman's voice called Sonny's name and a few hands started clapping. And Sonny, also being funny and being ceremonious, and so touched, I think, that he could have cried, but neither hiding it nor showing it, riding it like a man, grinned, and put both hands to his heart and bowed from the waist.

Creole then went to the bass fiddle and a lean, very bright-skinned brown man jumped up on the bandstand and picked up his horn. So there they were, and the atmosphere on the bandstand and in the room began to change and tighten. Someone stepped up to the microphone and announced them. Then there were all kinds of murmurs. Some people at the bar shushed others. The waitress ran around, frantically getting in the last orders, guys and chicks got closer to each other, and the lights on the bandstand, on the quartet, turned to a kind of indigo. Then they all looked different there. Creole looked about him for the last time, as though he were making certain that all his chickens were in the coop, and then he— jumped and struck the fiddle. And there they were.

All I know about music is that not many people ever really hear it. And even then, on the rare occasions when something opens within, and the music enters, what we mainly hear, or hear corroborated, are personal, private, vanishing evocations. But the man who creates the music is hearing something else, is dealing with the roar rising from the void and imposing order on it as it hits the air. What is evoked in him, then, is of another order, more terrible because it has no words, and triumphant, too, for that same reason. And his triumph, when he triumphs, is ours. I just watched Sonny's face. His face was troubled, he was working hard, but he wasn't with it. And I had the feeling that, in a way, everyone on the bandstand was waiting for him, both waiting for him and pushing him along. But as I began to watch Creole, I realized that it was Creole who held them all back. He had them on a short rein. Up there, keeping the beat with his whole body, wailing on the fiddle, with his eyes half closed, he was listening to everything, but he was listening to Sonny. He was having a dialogue with Sonny. He wanted Sonny to leave the shoreline and strike out for the deep water. He was Sonny's witness that deep water and drowning were not the same thing—he had been there, and he knew. And he wanted Sonny to know. He was waiting for Sonny to do the things on the keys which would let Creole know that Sonny was in the water.

And, while Creole listened, Sonny moved, deep within, exactly like someone in torment. I had never before thought of how awful the relationship must be between the musician and his instrument. He has to fill it, this instrument, with the breath of life, his own. He has to make it do what he wants it to do. And a piano is just a piano. It's made out of so much wood and wires and little hammers and big ones, and ivory. While there's only so much you can do with it, the only way to find this out is to try; to try and make it do everything.

And Sonny hadn't been near a piano for over a year. And he wasn't on much better terms with his life, not the life that stretched before him now. He and the piano stammered, started one way, got scared, stopped; started another way, panicked, marked time, started again; then seemed to have found a direction, panicked again, got stuck. And the face I saw on Sonny I'd never seen before. Everything had been burned out of it, and, at the same time, things usually hidden were being burned in, by the fire and fury of the battle which was occurring in him up there.

Yet, watching Creole's face as they neared the end of the first set, I had the feeling that something had happened, something I hadn't heard. Then they finished, there was scattered applause, and then, without an instant's warning, Creole started into something else, it was almost sardonic, it was *Am I Blue*. And, as though he commanded, Sonny began to play. Something began to happen. And Creole let out the reins. The dry, low, black man said something awful on the drums, Creole answered, and the drums talked back. Then the horn insisted, sweet and high, slightly detached perhaps, and Creole listened, commenting now and then, dry, and driving, beautiful and calm and old. Then they all came together again, and Sonny was part of the family again. I could tell this from his face. He seemed to have found, right there beneath his fingers, a damn brand-new piano. It seemed that he couldn't get over it. Then, for a while, just being happy with Sonny, they seemed to be agreeing with him that brand-new pianos certainly were a gas.

Then Creole stepped forward to remind them that what they were playing was the blues. He hit something in all of them, he hit something in me, myself, and the music tightened and deepened, apprehension began to beat the air. Creole began to tell us what the blues were all about. They were not about anything very new. He and his boys up there were keeping it new, at the risk of ruin, destruction, madness, and death, in order to find new ways to make us listen. For, while the tale of how we suffer, and how we are delighted, and how we may triumph is never new, it always must be heard. There isn't any other tale to tell, it's the only light we've got in all this darkness.

And this tale, according to that face, that body, those strong hands on those strings, has another aspect in every country, and a new depth in every generation. Listen, Creole seemed to be saying, listen. Now these are Sonny's blues. He made the little black man on the drums know it, and the bright, brown man on the horn. Creole wasn't trying any longer to get Sonny in the water. He was wishing him Godspeed. Then he stepped back, very slowly, filling the air with the immense suggestion that Sonny speak for himself.

Then they all gathered around Sonny and Sonny played. Every now and again one of them seemed to say, amen. Sonny's fingers filled the air with life, his life. But that life contained so many others. And Sonny went all the way back, he really began with the spare, flat statement of the opening phrase of the song. Then he began to make it his. It was very beautiful because it wasn't hurried and it was no longer a lament. I seemed to hear with what burning he had made it his, with what burning we had yet to make it ours, how we could cease lamenting. Freedom lurked around us and I understood, at last, that he could help us to be free if we would listen, that he would never be free until we did. Yet, there was no battle in his face now. I heard what he had gone through, and would continue to go through until he came to rest in earth. He had made it his: that long line, of which we knew only Mama and Daddy. And he was giving it back, as everything must be given back, so that, passing through death, it can live forever. I saw my mother's face again, and felt, for the first time, how the stones of the road she had walked on must have bruised her feet. I saw the moonlit road where my father's brother died. And it brought something else back to me, and carried me past it, I saw my little girl again and felt Isabel's tears again, and I felt my own tears begin to rise. And I was yet aware that this was only a moment, that the world waited outside, as hungry as a tiger, and that trouble stretched above us, longer than the sky.

Then it was over. Creole and Sonny let out their breath, both soaking wet, and grinning. There was a lot of applause and some of it was real. In the dark, the girl came by and I asked her to take drinks to the bandstand. There was a long pause, while they talked up there in the indigo light and after a while I saw the girl put a Scotch and milk on top of the piano for Sonny. He didn't seem to notice it, but just before they started playing again, he sipped from it and looked toward me, and nodded. Then he put it back on top of the piano. For me, then, as they began to play again, it glowed and shook above my brother's head like the very cup of trembling.

NOBODY KNOWS MY NAME:
A Letter from the South

I walked down the street, didn't
    have on no hat,
Asking everybody I meet,
Where's my man at?
                                    —Ma Rainey

Negroes in the North are right when they refer to the South as the Old Country. A Negro born in the North who finds himself in the South is in a position similar to that of the son of the Italian emigrant who finds himself in Italy, near the village where his father first saw the light of day. Both are in countries they have never seen, but which they cannot fail to recognize. The landscape has always been familiar; the speech is archaic, but it rings a bell; and so do the ways of the people, though their ways are not his ways. Everywhere he turns, the revenant finds himself reflected. He sees himself as he was before he was born, perhaps; or as the man he would have become, had he actually been born in this place. He sees the world, from an angle odd indeed, in which his fathers awaited his arrival, perhaps in the very house in which he narrowly avoided being born. He sees, in effect, his ancestors, who, in everything they do and are, proclaim his inescapable identity. And the Northern Negro in the South sees, whatever he or anyone else may wish to believe, that his ancestors are both white and black. The white men, flesh of his flesh, hate him for that very reason. On the other hand, there is scarcely any way for him to join the black community in the South: for both he and this community are in the grip of the immense illusion that their state is more miserable than his own.

This illusion owes everything to the great American illusion that our state is a state to be envied by other people: we are powerful, and we are rich. But our power makes us uncomfortable and we handle it very ineptly. The principal effect of our material well-being has been to set the children's teeth on edge. If we ourselves were not so fond of this illusion, we might understand ourselves and other peoples better than we do, and be enabled to help them understand us. I am very often tempted to believe that this illusion is all that is left of the great dream that was to have become America; whether this is so or not, this illusion certainly prevents us from making America what we say we want it to be.

But let us put aside, for the moment, these subversive speculations. In the fall of last year, my plane hovered over the rust-red earth of Georgia. I was past thirty, and I had never seen this land before. I pressed my face against the window, watching the earth come closer; soon we were just above the tops of trees. I could not suppress the thought that this earth had acquired its color from the blood that had dripped down from these trees. My mind was filled with the image of a black man, younger than I, perhaps, or my own age, hanging from a tree, while white men watched him and cut his sex from him with a knife.

My father must have seen such sights—he was very old when he died—or heard of them, or had this danger touch him. The Negro poet I talked to in Washington, much younger than my father, perhaps twenty years older than myself, remembered such things very vividly, had a long tale to tell, and counseled me to think back on those days as a means of steadying the soul. I was to remember that time, whatever else it had failed to do, nevertheless had passed, that the situation, whether or not it was better, was certainly no longer the same. I was to remember that Southern Negroes had endured things I could not imagine; but this did not really place me at such a great disadvantage, since they clearly had been unable to imagine what awaited them in Harlem. I remembered the Scottsboro case, which I had followed as a child. I remembered Angelo Herndon and wondered, again, whatever had become of him. I remembered the soldier in uniform blinded by an enraged white man, just after the Second World War. There had been many such incidents after the

First War, which was one of the reasons I had been born in Harlem. I remembered Willie McGhee, Emmett Till, and the others. My younger brothers had visited Atlanta some years before. I remembered what they had told me about it. One of my brothers, in uniform, had had his front teeth kicked out by a white officer. I remembered my mother telling us how she had wept and prayed and tried to kiss the venom out of her suicidally embittered son. (She managed to do it, too; heaven only knows what she herself was feeling, whose father and brothers had lived and died down here.) I remembered myself as a very small boy, already so bitter about the pledge of allegiance that I could scarcely bring myself to say it, and never, never believed it.

I was, in short, but one generation removed from the South, which was now undergoing a new convulsion over whether black children had the same rights, or capacities, for education as did the children of white people. This is a criminally frivolous dispute, absolutely unworthy of this nation; and it is being carried on, in complete bad faith, by completely uneducated people. (We do not trust educated people and rarely, alas, produce them, for we do not trust the independence of mind which alone makes a genuine education possible.) Educated people, of any color, are so extremely rare that it is unquestionably one of the first tasks of a nation to open all of its schools to all of its citizens. But the dispute has

actually nothing to do with education, as some among
the eminently uneducated know. It has to do with political power and it has to do with sex. And this is a nation
which, most unluckily, knows very little about either.

The city of Atlanta, according to my notes, is "big,
wholly segregated, sprawling; population variously given
as six hundred thousand or one million, depending on
whether one goes beyond or remains within the city limits. Negroes 25 to 30 percent of the population. Racial
relations, on the record, can be described as fair, considering that this is the state of Georgia. Growing industrial
town. Racial relations manipulated by the mayor and a
fairly strong Negro middle class. This works mainly in the
areas of compromise and concession and has very little
effect on the bulk of the Negro population and none
whatever on the rest of the state. No integration, pending
or actual." Also, it seemed to me that the Negroes in Atlanta
were "very vividly *city* Negroes"—they seemed less patient
than their rural brethren, more dangerous, or at least more
unpredictable. And: "Have seen one wealthy Negro section, very pretty, but with an unpaved road. . . . The section in which I am living is composed of frame houses in
various stages of disrepair and neglect, in which two and
three families live, often sharing a single toilet. This is the
other side of the tracks; literally, I mean. It is located, as I
am told is the case in many Southern cities, just beyond
the underpass." Atlanta contains a high proportion of

Negroes who own their own homes and exist, visibly anyway, independently of the white world. Southern towns
distrust this class and do everything in their power to prevent its appearance. But it is a class which has a certain
usefulness in Southern cities. There is an incipient war,
in fact, between Southern cities and Southern towns—
between the city, that is, and the state—which we will
discuss later. Little Rock is an ominous example of this and
it is likely—indeed, it is certain—that we will see many
more such examples before the present crisis is over.

Before arriving in Atlanta I had spent several days in
Charlotte, North Carolina. This is a bourgeois town, Presbyterian, pretty—if you like towns—and socially so her-
metic that it contains scarcely a single decent restaurant. I
was told that Negroes there are not even licensed to become
electricians or plumbers. I was also told, several times, by
white people, that "race relations" there were excellent. I
failed to find a single Negro who agreed with this, which
is the usual story of "race relations" in this country. Charlotte, a town of 165,000, was in a ferment when I was there
because, of its 50,000 Negroes, four had been assigned to
previously all-white schools, one to each school. In fact,
by the time I got there, there were only three. Dorothy
Counts, the daughter of a Presbyterian minister, after
several days of being stoned and spat on by the mob—
"spit," a woman told me, "was hanging from the hem of
Dorothy's dress"—had withdrawn from Harding High.

Several white students, I was told, had called—not called *on*—Miss Counts, to beg her to stick it out. Harry Golden, editor of *The Carolina Israelite*, suggested that the "hoodlum element" might not so have shamed the town and the nation if several of the town's leading businessmen had personally escorted Miss Counts to school.

I saw the Negro schools in Charlotte, saw, on street corners, several of their alumnae, and read about others who had been sentenced to the chain gang. This solved the mystery of just what made Negro parents send their children out to face mobs. White people do not understand this because they do not know, and do not want to know, that the alternative to this ordeal is nothing less than a lifelong ordeal. Those Negro parents who spend their days trembling for their children and the rest of their time praying that their children have not been too badly damaged inside, are not doing this out of "ideals" or "convictions" or because they are in the grip of a perverse desire to send their children where "they are not wanted." They are doing it because they want the child to receive the education which will allow him to defeat, possibly escape, and not impossibly help one day abolish the stifling environment in which they see, daily, so many children perish.

This is certainly not the purpose, still less the effect, of most Negro schools. It is hard enough, God knows, under the best of circumstances, to get an education in this country. White children are graduated yearly who can neither read, write, nor think, and who are in a state of the most abysmal ignorance concerning the world around them. But at least they are white. They are under the illusion—which, since they are so badly educated, sometimes has a fatal tenacity—that they can do whatever they want to do. Perhaps that is exactly what they *are* doing, in which case we had best all go down in prayer.

The level of Negro education, obviously, is even lower than the general level. The general level is low because, as I have said, Americans have so little respect for genuine intellectual effort. The Negro level is low because the education of Negroes occurs in, and is designed to perpetuate, a segregated society. This, in the first place, and no matter how much money the South boasts of spending on Negro schools, is utterly demoralizing. It creates a situation in which the Negro teacher is soon as powerless as his students. (There are exceptions among the teachers as there are among the students, but, in this country surely, schools have not been built for the exceptional. And, though white people often seem to expect Negroes to produce nothing but exceptions, the fact is that Negroes are really just like everybody else. Some of them are exceptional and most of them are not.)

The teachers are answerable to the Negro principal, whose power over the teachers is absolute but whose power with the school board is slight. As for this principal, he has arrived at the summit of his career; rarely indeed can he go any higher. He has his pension to look forward to, and he consoles himself, meanwhile, with his status among the "better class of Negroes." This class includes few, if any, of his students and by no means all of his teachers. The teachers, as long as they remain in this school system, and they certainly do not have much choice, can only aspire to become the principal one day. Since not all of them will make it, a great deal of the energy which ought to go into their vocation goes into the usual bitter, purposeless rivalry. They are underpaid and ill treated by the white world and rubbed raw by it every day; and it is altogether understandable that they, very shortly, cannot bear the sight of their students. The children know this; it is hard to fool young people. They also know why they are going to an overcrowded, outmoded plant, in classes so large that even the most strictly attentive student, the most gifted teacher cannot but feel himself slowly drowning in the sea of general helplessness.

It is not to be wondered at, therefore, that the violent distractions of puberty, occurring in such a cage, annually take their toll, sending female children into the maternity wards and male children into the streets. It is not to be wondered at that a boy, one day, decides that if all this studying is going to prepare him only to be a porter or an elevator boy—or his teacher—well, then, the hell with it. And there they go, with an overwhelming bitterness which they will dissemble all their lives, an unceasing effort which completes their ruin. They become the menial or the criminal or the shiftless, the Negroes whom segregation has produced and whom the South uses to prove that segregation is right.

In Charlotte, too, I received some notion of what the South means by "time to adjust." The NAACP there had been trying for six years before Black Monday to make the city fathers honor the "separate but equal" statute and do something about the situation in Negro schools. Nothing whatever was done. After Black Monday, Charlotte begged for "time": and what she did with this time was work out legal stratagems designed to get the least possible integration over the longest possible period. In August of 1955, Governor Hodges, a moderate, went on the air with the suggestion that Negroes segregate themselves voluntarily—for the good, as he put it, of both races. Negroes seeming to be unmoved by this moderate proposal, the Klan reappeared in the counties and was still active there when I left. So, no doubt, are the boys on the chain gang.

But "Charlotte," I was told, "is not the South." I was told, "You haven't seen the South yet." Charlotte seemed quite Southern enough for me, but, in fact, the people in Charlotte were right. One of the reasons for this is that the South is not the monolithic structure which, from the North, it appears to be, but a most various and divided region. It clings to the myth of its past but it is being inexorably changed, meanwhile, by an entirely unmythi-

cal present: its habits and its self-interest are at war. Everyone in the South feels this and this is why there is such
panic on the bottom and such impotence on the top.

It must also be said that the racial setup in the South is
not, for a Negro, very different from the racial setup in
the North. It is the etiquette which is baffling, not the
spirit. Segregation is unofficial in the North and official in
the South, a crucial difference that does nothing, nevertheless, to alleviate the lot of most Northern Negroes.
But we will return to this question when we discuss the
relationship between the Southern cities and states.

Atlanta, however, *is* the South. It is the South in this
respect, that it has a very bitter interracial history. This is
written in the faces of the people and one feels it in the
air. It was on the outskirts of Atlanta that I first felt how
the Southern landscape—the trees, the silence, the liquid
heat, and the fact that one always seems to be traveling
great distances—seems designed for violence, seems,
almost, to demand it. What passions cannot be unleashed
on a dark road in a Southern night! Everything seems so
sensual, so languid, and so private. Desire can be acted out
here; over this fence, behind that tree, in the darkness,
there; and no one will see, no one will ever know. Only
the night is watching and the night was made for desire.
Protestantism is the wrong religion for people in such cli-
mates; America is perhaps the last nation in which such a
climate belongs. In the Southern night everything seems

possible, the most private, unspeakable longings; but then arrives the Southern day, as hard and brazen as the night was soft and dark. It brings what was done in the dark to light. It must have seemed something like this for those people who made the region what it is today. It must have caused them great pain. Perhaps the master who had coupled with his slave saw his guilt in his wife's pale eyes in the morning. And the wife saw his children in the slave quarters, saw the way his concubine, the sensual-looking black girl, looked at her—a woman, after all, and scarcely less sensual, but white. The youth, nursed and raised by the black Mammy whose arms had then held all that there was of warmth and love and desire, and still confounded by the dreadful taboos set up between himself and her progeny, must have wondered, after his first experiment with black flesh, where, under the blazing heavens, he could hide. And the white man must have seen his guilt written somewhere else, seen it all the time, even if his sin was merely lust, even if his sin lay in nothing but his power: in the eyes of the black man. He may not have stolen his woman, but he had certainly stolen his freedom—this black man, who had a body like his, and passions like his, and a ruder, more erotic beauty. How many times has the Southern day come up to find that black man, sexless, hanging from a tree!

It was an old black man in Atlanta who looked into my eyes and directed me into my first segregated bus. I have spent a long time thinking about that man. I never saw him again. I cannot describe the look which passed between us, as I asked him for directions, but it made me think, at once, of Shakespeare's "the oldest have borne most." It made me think of the blues: *Now, when a woman gets the blues, Lord, she hangs her head and cries. But when a man gets the blues, Lord, he grabs a train and rides.* It was borne in on me, suddenly, just why these men had so often been grabbing freight trains as the evening sun went down. And it was, perhaps, because I was getting on a segregated bus, and wondering how Negroes had borne this and other indignities for so long, that this man so struck me. He seemed to know what I was feeling. His eyes seemed to say that what I was feeling he had been feeling, at much higher pressure, all his life. But my eyes would never see the hell his eyes had seen. And this hell was, simply, that he had never in his life owned anything, not his wife, not his house, not his child, which could not, at any instant, be taken from him by the power of white people. This is what paternalism means. And for the rest of the time that I was in the South I watched the eyes of old black men.

Atlanta's well-to-do Negroes never take buses, for they all have cars. The section in which they live is quite far away from the poor Negro section. They own, or at least are paying for, their own homes. They drive to work and back, and have cocktails and dinner with each other. They see very little of the white world; but they are cut off from the black world, too.

Now, of course, this last statement is not literally true. The teachers teach Negroes, the lawyers defend them. The ministers preach to them and bury them, and others insure their lives, pull their teeth, and cure their ailments. Some of the lawyers work with the NAACP and help push test cases through the courts. (If anything, by the way, disproves the charge of "extremism" which has so often been made against this organization, it is the fantastic care and patience such legal efforts demand.) Many of the teachers work very hard to bolster the morale of their students and prepare them for their new responsibilities; nor did those I met fool themselves about the hideous system under which they work. So when I say that they are cut off from the black world, I am not sneering, which, indeed, I scarcely have any right to do. I am talking about their position as a class—*if* they are a class—and their role in a very complex and shaky social structure.

The wealthier Negroes are, at the moment, very useful for the administration of the city of Atlanta, for they represent there the potential, at least, of interracial communication. That this phrase is a euphemism, in Atlanta as elsewhere, becomes clear when one considers how astonishingly little has been communicated in all these generations. What the phrase almost always has reference to is the fact that, in a given time and place, the Negro vote is of sufficient value to force politicians to bargain for it. What interracial communication also refers to is that Atlanta is really growing and thriving, and because it wants to make even more money, it would like to prevent incidents that disturb the peace, discourage investments, and permit test cases, which the city of Atlanta would certainly lose, to come to the courts. Once this happens, as it certainly will one day, the state of Georgia will be up in arms and the present administration of the city will be out of power. I did not meet a soul in Atlanta (I naturally did not meet any members of the White Citizen's Council, not, anyway, to talk to) who did not pray that the present mayor would be reelected. Not that they loved him particularly, but it is his administration which holds off the holocaust.

Now this places Atlanta's wealthy Negroes in a really quite sinister position. Though both they and the mayor are devoted to keeping the peace, their aims and his are not, and cannot be, the same. Many of those lawyers are working day and night on test cases which the mayor is doing his best to keep out of court. The teachers spend their working day attempting to destroy in their students—and it is not too much to say, in themselves—those habits of inferiority which form one of the principal cornerstones of segregation as it is practiced in the South. Many of the parents listen to speeches by people like Senator

Russell and find themselves unable to sleep at night. They are in the extraordinary position of being compelled to work for the destruction of all they have bought so dearly—their homes, their comfort, the safety of their children. But the safety of their children is merely comparative; it is all that their comparative strength as a class has bought them so far; and they are not safe, really, as long as the bulk of Atlanta's Negroes live in such darkness. On any night, in that other part of town, a policeman may beat up one Negro too many, or some Negro or some white man may simply go berserk. This is all it takes to drive so delicately balanced a city mad. And the island on which these Negroes have built their handsome houses will simply disappear.

This is not at all in the interests of Atlanta, and almost everyone there knows it. Left to itself, the city might grudgingly work out compromises designed to reduce the tension and raise the level of Negro life. But it is not left to itself; it belongs to the state of Georgia. The Negro vote has no power in the state, and the governor of Georgia—that "third-rate man," Atlantans call him—makes great political capital out of keeping the Negroes in their place. When six Negro ministers attempted to create a test case by ignoring the segregation ordinance on the buses, the governor was ready to declare martial law and hold the ministers incommunicado. It was the mayor who prevented this, who somehow squashed all publicity, treated the ministers with every outward sign of respect, and it is his office which is preventing the case from coming into court. And remember that it was the governor of Arkansas, in an insane bid for political power, who created the present crisis in Little Rock—against the will of most of its citizens and against the will of the mayor.

This war between the Southern cities and states is of the utmost importance, not only for the South, but for the nation. The Southern states are still very largely governed by people whose political lives, insofar, at least, as they are able to conceive of life or politics, are dependent on the people in the rural regions. It might, indeed, be more honorable to try to guide these people out of their pain and ignorance instead of locking them within it, and battening on it; but it is, admittedly, a difficult task to try to tell people the truth and it is clear that most Southern politicians have no intention of attempting it. The attitude of these people can only have the effect of stiffening the already implacable Negro resistance, and this attitude is absolutely certain, sooner or later, to create great trouble in the cities. When a race riot occurs in Atlanta, it will not spread merely to Birmingham, for example. (Birmingham is a doomed city.) The trouble will spread to every metropolitan center in the nation which has a significant Negro population. And this is not only because the ties between Northern and Southern Negroes are still very close. It is because the nation, the entire nation, has spent a hundred years avoiding the question of the place of the black man in it.

That this has done terrible things to black men is not even a question. "Integration," said a very light Negro to me in Alabama, "has always worked very well in the South, after the sun goes down." "It's not miscegenation," said another Negro to me, "unless a black man's involved." Now, I talked to many Southern liberals who were doing their best to bring integration about in the South, but met scarcely a single Southerner who did not weep for the passing of the old order. They were perfectly sincere, too, and, within their limits, they were right. They pointed out how Negroes and whites in the South had loved each other, they recounted to me tales of devotion and heroism which the old order had produced, and which, now, would never come again. But the old black men I looked at down there—those same black men that the Southern liberal had loved; for whom, until now, the Southern liberal—and not only the liberal—has been willing to undergo great inconvenience and danger—they were not weeping. Men do not like to be protected, it emasculates them. This is what black men know, it is the reality they have lived with; it is what white men do not want to know. It is not a pretty thing to be a father and be ultimately dependent on the power and kindness of some other man for the well-being of your house.

But what this evasion of the Negro's humanity has

done to the nation is not so well known. The really striking thing, for me, in the South was this dreadful paradox,
that the black men were stronger than the white. I do
not know how they did it, but it certainly has something
to do with that as yet unwritten history of the Negro
woman. What it comes to, finally, is that the nation has
spent a large part of its time and energy looking away
from one of the principal facts of its life. This failure to
look reality in the face diminishes a nation as it diminishes
a person, and it can only be described as unmanly. And in
exactly the same way that the South imagines that it
"knows" the Negro, the North imagines that it has set
him free. Both camps are deluded. Human freedom is a
complex, difficult—and private—thing. If we can liken
life, for a moment, to a furnace, then freedom is the fire
which burns away illusion. Any honest examination of
the national life proves how far we are from the standard
of human freedom with which we began. The recovery
of this standard demands of everyone who loves this
country a hard look at himself, for the greatest achieve-
ments must begin somewhere, and they always begin
with the person. If we are not capable of this examination, we may yet become one of the most distinguished
and monumental failures in the history of nations.

He was facing Seventh Avenue, at Times Square. It was past midnight and he had been sitting in the movies, in the top row of the balcony, since two o'clock in the afternoon. Twice he had been awakened by the violent accents of the Italian film, once the usher had awakened him, and twice he had been awakened by caterpillar fingers between his thighs. He was so tired, he had fallen so low, that he scarcely had the energy to be angry; nothing of his belonged to him anymore—*you took the best, so why not take the rest?*—but he had growled in his sleep and bared the white teeth in his dark face and crossed his legs. Then the balcony was nearly empty, the Italian film was approaching a climax; he stumbled down the endless stairs into the street. He was hungry, his mouth felt filthy. He realized too late, as he passed through the doors, that he

wanted to urinate. And he was broke. And he had nowhere
to go.

The policeman passed him, giving him a look. Rufus
turned, pulling up the collar of his leather jacket while
the wind nibbled delightedly at him through his summer
slacks, and started north on Seventh Avenue. He had been
thinking of going downtown and waking up Vivaldo—
the only friend he had left in the city, or maybe in the
world—but now he decided to walk up as far as a certain
jazz bar and night club and look in. Maybe somebody
would see him and recognize him, maybe one of the guys
would lay enough bread on him for a meal or at least subway fare. At the same time, he hoped that he would not
be recognized.

The Avenue was quiet, too, most of its bright lights out.
Here and there a woman passed, here and there a man;
rarely, a couple. At corners, under the lights, near drugstores, small knots of white, bright, chattering people
showed teeth to each other, pawed each other, whistled
for taxis, were whirled away in them, vanished through the
doors of drugstores or into the blackness of side streets.
Newsstands, like small black blocks on a board, held down
corners of the pavements and policemen and taxi drivers
and others, harder to place, stomped their feet before them
and exchanged such words as they both knew with the
muffled vendor within. A sign advertised the chewing gum
which would help one to relax and keep smiling. A hotel's

enormous neon name challenged the starless sky. So did the names of movie stars and people currently appearing or scheduled to appear on Broadway, along with the mile-high names of the vehicles which would carry them into immortality. The great buildings, unlit, blunt like the phallus or sharp like the spear, guarded the city which never slept.

Beneath them Rufus walked, one of the fallen—for the weight of this city was murderous—one of those who had been crushed on the day, which was every day, these towers fell. Entirely alone, and dying of it, he was part of an unprecedented multitude. There were boys and girls drinking coffee at the drugstore counters who were held back from his condition by barriers as perishable as their dwindling cigarettes. They could scarcely bear their knowledge, nor could they have borne the sight of Rufus, but they knew why he was in the streets tonight, why he rode subways all night long, why his stomach growled, why his hair was nappy, his armpits funky, his pants and shoes too thin, and why he did not dare to stop and take a leak.

Now he stood before the misty doors of the jazz joint, peering in, sensing rather than seeing the frantic black people on the stand and the oblivious, mixed crowd at the bar. The music was loud and empty, no one was doing anything at all, and it was being hurled at the crowd like a malediction in which not even those who hated most deeply any longer believed. They knew that no one heard, that bloodless people cannot be made to bleed. So they blew what everyone had heard before, they reassured everyone that nothing terrible was happening, and the people at the tables found it pleasant to shout over this stunning corroboration and the people at the bar, under cover of the noise they could scarcely have lived without, pursued whatever it was they were after. He wanted to go in and use the bathroom but he was ashamed of the way he looked. He had been in hiding, really, for nearly a month. And he saw himself now, in his mind's eye, shambling through this crowd to the bathroom and crawling out again while everyone watched him with pitying or scornful or mocking eyes. Or, someone would be certain to whisper *Isn't that Rufus Scott?* Someone would look at him with horror, then turn back to his business with a long-drawn-out, pitying, *Man!* He could not do it—and he danced on one foot and then the other and tears came to his eyes.

A white couple, laughing, came through the doors, giving him barely a glance as they passed. The warmth, the smell of people, whiskey, beer, and smoke which came out to hit him as the doors opened almost made him cry for fair and it made his empty stomach growl again.

It made him remember days and nights, days and nights, when he had been inside, on the stand or in the crowd, sharp, beloved, making it with any chick he wanted, making it to parties and getting high and getting drunk and fooling around with the musicians, who were his friends, who respected him. Then, going home to his own pad, locking his door and taking off his shoes, maybe making himself a drink, maybe listening to some records, stretching out on the bed, maybe calling up some girl. And changing his underwear and his socks and his shirt, shaving, and taking a shower, and making it to Harlem to the barber shop, then seeing his mother and his father and teasing his sister, Ida, and eating: spareribs or pork chops or chicken or greens or cornbread or yams or biscuits. For a moment he thought he would faint with hunger and he moved to a wall of the building and leaned there. His forehead was freezing with sweat. He thought: this is got to stop, Rufus. This shit is got to stop. Then, in weariness and recklessness, seeing no one on the streets and hoping that no one would come through the doors, leaning with one hand against the wall he sent his urine splashing against the stone-cold pavement, watching the faint steam rise.

He remembered Leona. Or a sudden, cold, familiar sickness filled him and he knew he was remembering Leona. And he began to walk, very slowly now, away from the music, with his hands in his pockets and his head down. He no longer felt the cold.

For to remember Leona was also—somehow—to remember the eyes of his mother, the rage of his father, the beauty of his sister. It was to remember the streets of Harlem, the boys on the stoops, the girls behind the stairs and on the roofs, the white policemen who had taught him how to hate, the stickball games in the streets, the women leaning out of windows and the numbers they played daily, hoping for the hit his father never made. It was to remember the juke box, the teasing, the dancing, the hard-on, the gang fights and gang bangs, his first set of drums—bought him by his father—his first taste of marijuana, his first snort of horse. Yes: and the boys too far out, jackknifed on the stoops, the boy dead from an overdose on a rooftop in the snow. It was to remember the beat: *A nigger,* said his father, *lives his whole life, lives and dies according to a beat. Shit, he humps to that beat and the baby he throws up in there, well, he jumps to it and comes out nine months later like a goddamn tambourine.* The beat: hands, feet, tambourines, drums, pianos, laughter, curses, razor blades; the man stiffening with a laugh and a growl and a purr and the woman moistening and softening with a whisper and a sigh and a cry. The beat—in Harlem in the summertime one could almost see it, shaking above the pavements and the roof.

And he had fled, so he had thought, from the beat of Harlem, which was simply the beat of his own heart. Into a boot camp in the South, and onto the pounding sea.

While he had still been in the navy, he had brought back from one of his voyages an Indian shawl for Ida. He had picked it up someplace in England. On the day that he gave it to her and she tried it on, something shook in him which had never been touched before. He had never seen the beauty of black people before. But, staring at Ida, who stood before the window of the Harlem kitchen, seeing that she was no longer merely his younger sister but a girl who would soon be a woman, she became associated with the colors of the shawl, the colors of the sun, and with a splendor incalculably older than the gray stone of the island on which they had been born. He thought that perhaps this splendor would come into the world again one day, into the world they knew. Ages and ages ago, Ida had not been merely the descendant of slaves. Watching her dark face in the sunlight, softened and shadowed by the glorious shawl, it could be seen that she had once been a monarch. Then he looked out of the window, at the air shaft, and thought of the whores on Seventh Avenue. He thought of the white policemen and the money they made on black flesh, the money the whole world made.

He looked back at his sister, who was smiling at him. On her long little finger she twisted the ruby-eyed snake ring which he had brought her from another voyage.

"You keep this up," she said, "and you'll make me the best-dressed girl on the block."

He was glad Ida could not see him now. She would have said, My Lord, Rufus, you got no right to walk around like this. Don't you know we're counting on you?

———

Seven months ago, a lifetime ago, he had been playing a gig in one of the new Harlem spots owned and operated by a Negro. It was their last night. It had been a good night, everybody was feeling good. Most of them, after the set, were going to make it to the home of a famous Negro singer who had just scored in his first movie. Because the joint was new, it was packed. Lately, he had heard, it hadn't been doing so well. All kinds of people had been there that night, white and black, high and low, people who came for the music and people who spent their lives in joints for other reasons. There were a couple of minks and a few near-minks and a lot of God-knows-what shining at wrists and ears and necks and in the hair. The colored people were having a good time because they sensed that, for whatever reason, this crowd was solidly with them; and the white people were having a good time because nobody was putting them down for being white. The joint, as Fats Waller would have said, was jumping.

There was some pot on the scene and he was a little high. He was feeling great. And, during the last set, he came doubly alive because the saxophone player, who had been way out all night, took off on a terrific solo. He was a kid of about the same age as Rufus, from some insane place like Jersey City or Syracuse, but somewhere along the line he had discovered that he could say it with a saxophone. He had a lot to say. He stood there, wide-legged, humping the air, filling his barrel chest, shivering in the rags of his twenty-odd years, and screaming through the horn *Do you love me? Do you love me? Do you love me?* And, again, Do *you love me? Do you* love *me? Do you love* me? This, anyway, was the question Rufus heard, the same phrase, unbearably, endlessly, and variously repeated, with all of the force the boy had. The silence of the listeners became strict with abruptly focused attention, cigarettes were unlit, and drinks stayed on the tables; and in all of the faces, even the most ruined and most dull, a curious, wary light appeared. They were being assaulted by the saxophonist who perhaps no longer wanted their love and merely hurled his outrage at them with the same contemptuous, pagan pride with which he humped the air. And yet the question was terrible and real; the boy was blowing with his lungs and guts out of his own short past; somewhere in that past, in the gutters or gang fights or gang shags; in the acrid room, on the sperm-stiffened blanket, behind marijuana or the needle, under the smell of piss in the precinct basement, he had received the blow from which he never would recover and this no one wanted to believe. *Do you love me? Do you love me? Do you love* me? The men on the stand stayed with him, cool and at a little distance, adding and questioning and corroborating, holding it down as well as they could with an ironical self-mockery; but each man knew that the boy was blowing for every one of them. When the set ended they were all soaking. Rufus smelled his odor and the odor of the men around him and "Well, that's it," said the bass man. The crowd was yelling for more but they did their theme song and the lights came on. And he had played the last set of his last gig.

He was going to leave his traps there until Monday afternoon. When he stepped down from the stand there was this blond girl, very plainly dressed, standing looking at him.

"What's on your mind, baby?" he asked her. Everybody was busy all around them, preparing to make it to the party. It was spring and the air was charged.

"What's on *your* mind?" she countered, but it was clear that she simply had not known what else to say.

She had said enough. She was from the South. And something leaped in Rufus as he stared at her damp, colorless face, the face of the Southern poor white, and her straight, pale hair. She was considerably older than he, over thirty probably, and her body was too thin. Just the same, it abruptly became the most exciting body he had gazed on in a long time.

"Honeychild," he said and gave her his crooked grin, "ain't you a long ways from home?"

"I sure am," she said, "and I ain't never going back there."

He laughed and she laughed. "Well, Miss Anne," he said, "if we both got the same thing on our mind, let's make it to that party."

And he took her arm, deliberately allowing the back of

his hand to touch one of her breasts, and he said, "Your name's not really Anne, is it?"

"No," she said, "it's Leona."

"Leona?" And he smiled again. His smile could be very effective. "That's a pretty name."

"What's yours?"

"Me? I'm Rufus Scott."

He wondered what she was doing in this joint, in Harlem. She didn't seem at all the type to be interested in jazz, still less did she seem to be in the habit of going to strange bars alone. She carried a light spring coat, her long hair was simply brushed back and held with some pins, she wore very little lipstick and no other make-up at all.

"Come on," he said. "We'll pile into a cab."

"Are you sure it's all right if I come?"

He sucked his teeth. "If it wasn't all right, I wouldn't ask you. If I say it's all right, it's all *right*."

"Well," she said with a short laugh, "all right, then."

They moved with the crowd, which, with many interruptions, much talking and laughing and much erotic confusion, poured into the streets. It was three o'clock in the morning and gala people all around them were glittering and whistling and using up all the taxicabs. Others, considerably less gala—they were on the western edge of 125th Street—stood in knots along the street, switched or swaggered or dawdled by, with glances, sidelong or full face, which were more calculating than curious. The

policemen strolled by; carefully, and in fact rather mysteriously conveying their awareness that these particular
Negroes, though they were out so late, and mostly drunk,
were not to be treated in the usual fashion; and neither
were the white people with them. But Rufus suddenly
realized that Leona would soon be the only white person
left. This made him uneasy and his uneasiness made him
angry. Leona spotted an empty cab and hailed it.

The taxi driver, who was white, seemed to have no hesi-
tation in stopping for them, nor, once having stopped, did
he seem to have any regrets.

"You going to work tomorrow?" he asked Leona.
Now that they were alone together, he felt a little shy.

"No," she said, "tomorrow's Sunday."

"That's right." He felt very pleased and free. He had
planned to visit his family but he thought of what a ball
it would be to spend the day in bed with Leona. He
glanced over at her, noting that, though she was tiny, she
seemed very well put together. He wondered what she
was thinking. He offered her a cigarette putting his hand
on hers briefly, and she refused it. "You don't smoke?"

"Sometimes. When I drink."

"Is that often?"

She laughed. "No. I don't like to drink alone."

"Well," he said, "you ain't *going* to be drinking alone
for a while."

She said nothing but she seemed, in the darkness, to

tense and blush. She looked out of the window on her side. "I'm glad I ain't got to worry none about getting you home early tonight."

"You ain't got to worry about that, nohow. I'm a big girl."

"Honey," he said, "you ain't no bigger than a minute."

She sighed. "Sometimes a minute can be a mighty powerful thing."

He decided against asking what she meant by this. He said, giving her a significant look, "That's true," but she did not seem to take his meaning.

They were on Riverside Drive and nearing their destination. To the left of them, pale, unlovely lights emphasized the blackness of the Jersey shore. He leaned back, leaning a little against Leona, watching the blackness and the lights roll by. Then the cab turned; he glimpsed, briefly, the distant bridge which glowed like something written in the sky. The cab slowed down, looking for the house number. A taxi ahead of them had just discharged a crowd of people and was disappearing down the block. "Here we are," said Rufus; "Looks like a real fine party," the taxi driver said, and winked. Rufus said nothing. He paid the man and they got out and walked into the lobby, which was large and hideous, with mirrors and chairs. The elevator had just started upward; they could hear the crowd.

"What were you doing in that club all by yourself, Leona?" he asked.

She looked at him, a little startled. Then, "I don't know. I just wanted to see Harlem and so I went up there tonight to look around. And I just happened to pass that club and I heard the music and I went in and I *stayed*. I liked the music." She gave him a mocking look. "Is that all right?"

He laughed and said nothing.

She turned from him as they heard the sound of the closing elevator door reverberate down the shaft. Then they heard the drone of the cables as the elevator began to descend. She watched the closed doors as though her life depended on it.

"This your first time in New York?"

Yes, it was, she told him, but she had been dreaming about it all her life—half-facing him again, with a little smile. There was something halting in her manner which he found very moving. She was like a wild animal who didn't know whether to come to the outstretched hand or to flee and kept making startled little rushes, first in one direction and then in the other.

"I was born here," he said, watching her.

"I know," she said, "so it can't seem as wonderful to you as it does to me."

He laughed again. He remembered, suddenly, his days in boot camp in the South and felt again the shoe of a white officer against his mouth. He was in his white uniform, on the ground, against the red, dusty clay. Some of his colored buddies were holding him, were shouting in his ear, helping him to rise. The white officer, with a curse, had vanished, had gone forever beyond the reach of vengeance. His face was full of clay and tears and blood; he spat red blood into the red dust.

The elevator came and the doors opened. He took her arm as they entered and held it close against his chest. "I think you're a real sweet girl."

"You're nice, too," she said. In the closed, rising elevator her voice had a strange trembling in it and her body was also trembling—very faintly, as though it were being handled by the soft spring wind outside.

He tightened his pressure on her arm. "Didn't they warn you down home about the darkies you'd find up North?"

She caught her breath. "They didn't never worry me none. People's just people as far as I'm concerned."

And pussy's just pussy as far as I'm concerned, he thought—but was grateful, just the same, for her tone. It gave him an instant to locate himself. For he, too, was trembling slightly.

"What made you come North?" he asked.

He wondered if he should proposition her or wait for her to proposition him. He couldn't beg. But perhaps she could. The hairs of his groin began to itch slightly. The terrible muscle at the base of his belly began to grow hot and hard.

The elevator came to a halt, the doors opened, and they walked a long corridor toward a half-open door.

She said, "I guess I just couldn't take it down there any more. I was married but then I broke up with my husband and they took away my kid—they wouldn't even let me see him—and I got to thinking that rather than sit down there and go crazy, I'd try to make a new life for myself up here."

Something touched his imagination for a moment, suggesting that Leona was a person and had her story and that all stories were trouble. But he shook the suggestion off. He wouldn't be around long enough to be bugged by her story. He just wanted her for tonight.

He knocked on the door and walked in without waiting for an answer. Straight ahead of them, in the large living room which ended in open French doors and a balcony, more than a hundred people milled about, some in evening dress, some in slacks and sweaters. High above their heads hung an enormous silver ball which reflected unexpected parts of the room and managed its own unloving comment on the people in it. The room was so active with coming and going, so bright with jewelry and glasses and cigarettes, that the heavy ball seemed almost to be alive.

His host—whom he did not really know very well—was nowhere in sight. To the right of them were three rooms, the first of which was piled high with wraps and overcoats.

The horn of Charlie Parker, coming over the hi-fi, dominated all the voices in the room.

"Put your coat down," he told Leona, "and I'll try to find out if I know anybody in this joint."

"Oh," she said, "I'm sure you know them all."

"Go on, now," he said, smiling, and pushing her gently into the room, "do like I tell you."

While she was putting away her coat—and powdering her nose, probably—he remembered that he had promised to call Vivaldo. He wandered through the house, looking for a relatively isolated telephone, and found one in the kitchen.

He dialed Vivaldo's number.

"Hello, baby. How're you?"

"Oh, all right, I guess. What's happening? I thought you were going to call me sooner. I'd just about given you up."

"Well, I only just made it up here." He dropped his voice, for a couple had entered the kitchen, a blond girl with a disarrayed Dutch bob and a tall Negro. The girl leaned against the sink, the boy stood before her, rubbing his hands slowly along the outside of her thighs. They barely glanced at Rufus. "A whole lot of elegant squares around, you dig?"

"Yeah," said Vivaldo. There was a pause. "You think it's worthwhile making it up there?"

"Well, hell, I don't know. If you got something *better* to do—"

"Jane's here," Vivaldo said, quickly. Rufus realized that Jane was probably lying on the bed, listening.

"Oh, you got your grandmother with you, you don't

need nothing up here then." He did not like Jane, who was somewhat older than Vivaldo, with prematurely gray hair. "Ain't nothing up here old enough for you."

"That's enough, you bastard." He heard Jane's voice and Vivaldo's, murmuring; he could not make out what was being said. Then Vivaldo's voice was at his ear again. "I think I'll skip it."

"I guess you better. I'll see you tomorrow."

"Maybe I'll come by your pad—?"

"Okay. Don't let grandma wear you out now; they tell me women get real ferocious when they get as old as she is."

"They can't get too ferocious for me, dad!"

Rufus laughed. "You better *quit* trying to compete with me. *You* ain't never going to make it. So long."

"So long."

He hung up, smiling, and went to find Leona. She stood helplessly in the foyer, watching the host and hostess saying good night to several people.

"Think I'd deserted you?"

"No. I knew you wouldn't do that."

He smiled at her and touched her on the chin with his fist. The host turned away from the door and came over to them.

"You kids go inside and get yourselves a drink," he said. "Go on in and get with it." He was a big, handsome, expansive man, older and more ruthless than he looked, who had fought his way to the top in show business via several of the rougher professions, including boxing and pimping. He owed his present eminence more to his vitality and his looks than he did to his voice, and he knew it. He was not the kind of man who fooled himself and Rufus liked him because he was rough and good-natured and generous. But Rufus was also a little afraid of him; there was that about him, in spite of his charm, which did not encourage intimacy. He was a great success with women, whom he treated with a large, affectionate contempt, and he was now on his fourth wife.

He took Leona and Rufus by the arm and walked them to the edge of the party. "We might have us some real doings if these squares ever get out of here," he said. "Stick around."

"How does it feel to be respectable?" Rufus grinned.

"Shit. I been respectable all my life. It's these *respectable* motherfuckers been doing all the dirt. They been stealing the colored folks blind, man. And niggers helping them do it." He laughed. "You know, every time they give me one of them great big checks I think to myself, they just giving me back a *little* bit of what they been stealing all these years, you know what I mean?" He clapped Rufus on the back. "See that Little Eva has a good time."

The crowd was already thinning, most of the squares were beginning to drift away. Once they were gone, the party would change character and become very pleasant and quiet and private. The lights would go down, the music become softer, the talk more sporadic and more sincere. Somebody might sing or play the piano. They might swap stories of the laughs they'd had, gigs they'd played, riffs they remembered, or the trouble they'd seen. Somebody might break out with some pot and pass it slowly around, like the pipe of peace. Somebody, curled on a rug in a far corner of the room, would begin to snore. Whoever danced would dance more languorously, holding tight. The shadows of the room would be alive. Toward the very end, as morning and the brutal sounds of the city began their invasion through the wide French doors, somebody would go into the kitchen and break out with some coffee. Then they would raid the icebox and go home. The host and hostess would finally make it between their sheets and stay in bed all day.

From time to time Rufus found himself glancing upward at the silver ball in the ceiling, always just failing to find himself and Leona reflected there.

"Let's go out to the balcony," he said to her.

She held out her glass. "Freshen my drink first?" Her eyes were now very bright and mischievous and she looked like a little girl.

He walked to the table and poured two very powerful drinks. He went back to her. "Ready?"

She took her glass and they stepped through the French doors.

"Don't let Little Eva catch cold!" the host called.

He called back. "She may burn, baby, but she sure won't freeze!"

Directly before and beneath them stretched the lights of the Jersey shore. He seemed, from where he stood, to hear a faint murmur coming from the water.

When a child he had lived on the eastern edge of Harlem, a block from the Harlem River. He and other children had waded into the water from the garbage-heavy bank or dived from occasional rotting promontories. One summer a boy had drowned there. From the stoop of his house Rufus had watched as a small group of people crossed Park Avenue, beneath the heavy shadow of the railroad tracks, and come into the sun, one man in the middle, the boy's father, carrying the boy's unbelievably heavy, covered weight. He had never forgotten the bend of the man's shoulders or the stunned angle of his head. A great screaming began from the other end of the block and the boy's mother, her head tied up, wearing her bathrobe, stumbling like a drunken woman, began running toward the silent people.

He threw back his shoulders, as though he were casting off a burden, and walked to the edge of the balcony where Leona stood. She was staring up the river, toward the George Washington Bridge.

"It's real beautiful," she said, "it's just so beautiful."

"You seem to like New York," he said.

She turned and looked at him and sipped her drink. "Oh, I do. Can I trouble you for a cigarette now?"

He gave her a cigarette and lit it for her, then lit one for himself. "How're you making it up here?"

"Oh, I'm doing just fine," she said. "I'm waiting tables in a restaurant way downtown, near Wall Street, that's a real pretty part of town, and I'm rooming with two other girls"—they couldn't go to *her* place, anyway!—"and, oh, I'm doing just fine." And she looked up at him with her sad-sweet, poor-white smile.

Again something warned him to stop, to leave this poor little girl alone; and at the same time the fact that he thought of her as a poor little girl caused him to smile with real affection, and he said, "You've got a lot of guts, Leona."

"Got to, the way I look at it," she said. "Sometimes I think I'll just give up. But—*how* do you give up?"

She looked so lost and comical that he laughed out loud and, after a moment, she laughed too.

"If my husband could see me now," and she giggled, "my, my, my!"

"Why, what would your husband say?" he asked her.

"Why—I don't know." But her laugh didn't come this time. She looked at him as though she were slowly coming out of a dream. "Say—do you think I could have another drink?"

"Sure, Leona," and he took her glass and their hands and their bodies touched for a moment. She dropped her eyes. "Be right back," he said, and dropped back into the room, in which the lights now were dim. Someone was playing the piano.

"Say, man, how you coming with Eva?" the host asked.

"Fine, fine, we lushing it up."

"That ain't nowhere. Blast Little Eva with some pot. Let her get her kicks."

"I'll see to it that she gets her kicks," he said.

"Old Rufus left her out there digging the Empire State building, man," said the young saxophonist, and laughed.

"Give me some of that," Rufus said, and somebody handed him a stick and he took a few drags.

"Keep it, man. It's choice."

He made a couple of drinks and stood in the room for a moment, finishing the pot and digging the piano. He felt fine, clean, on top of everything, and he had a mild buzz on when he got back to the balcony.

"Is everybody gone home?" she asked, anxiously. "It's so quiet in there."

"No," he said, "they just sitting around." She seemed prettier suddenly, and softer, and the river lights fell behind her like a curtain. This curtain seemed to move as she moved, heavy and priceless and dazzling. "I didn't know," he said, "that you were a princess."

He gave her her drink and their hands touched again. "I know you must be drunk," she said, happily, and now, over her drink, her eyes unmistakably called him.

He waited. Everything seemed very simple now. He played with her fingers. "You seen anything you want since you been in New York?"

"Oh," she said, "I want it all!"

"You see anything you want right now?"

Her fingers stiffened slightly but he held on. "Go ahead. Tell me. You ain't got to be afraid." These words then echoed in his head. He had said this before, years ago, to someone else. The wind grew cold for an instant, blowing around his body and ruffling her hair. Then it died down.

"Do *you*?" she asked faintly.

"Do I what?"

"See anything you want?"

He realized that he was high from the way his fingers seemed hung up in hers and from the way he was staring at her throat. He wanted to put his mouth there and nibble it slowly, leaving it black and blue. At the same time he realized how far they were above the city and the lights below seemed to be calling him. He walked to the balcony's edge and looked over. Looking straight down, he seemed to be standing on a cliff in the wilderness, seeing a kingdom and a river which had not been seen before. He could make it his, every inch of the territory which stretched beneath and around him now, and, unconsciously, he began whistling a tune and his foot moved to find the pedal of his drum. He put his drink down carefully on the balcony floor and beat a riff with his fingers on the stone parapet.

"You never answered my question."

"What?"

He turned to face Leona, who held her drink cupped in both her hands and whose brow was quizzically lifted over her despairing eyes and her sweet smile.

"You never answered mine."

"Yes, I did." She sounded more plaintive than ever. "I said I wanted it all."

He took her drink from her and drank half of it, then gave the glass back, moving into the darkest part of the balcony.

"Well, then," he whispered, "come and get it."

She came toward him, holding her glass against her breasts. At the very last moment, standing directly before him, she whispered in bafflement and rage, "What are you trying to do to me?"

"Honey," he answered, "I'm doing it," and he pulled her to him as roughly as he could. He had expected her to resist and she did, holding the glass between them and frantically trying to pull her body away from his body's touch. He knocked the glass out of her hand and it fell dully to the balcony floor, rolling away from them. Go ahead, he thought humorously; if I was to let you go now you'd be so hung up you'd go flying over this balcony, most likely. He whispered, "Go ahead, fight. I like it. Is this the way they do down home?"

"Oh God," she murmured, and began to cry. At the

same time, she ceased struggling. Her hands came up and touched his face as though she were blind. Then she put her arms around his neck and clung to him, still shaking. His lips and his teeth touched her ears and her neck and he told her. "Honey, you ain't got nothing to cry about yet."

Yes, he was high; everything he did he watched himself doing, and he began to feel a tenderness for Leona which he had not expected to feel. He tried, with himself, to make amends for what he was doing—for what he was doing to her. Everything seemed to take a very long time. He got hung up on her breasts, standing out like mounds of yellow cream, and the tough, brown, tasty nipples, playing and nuzzling and nibbling while she moaned and whimpered and her knees sagged. He gently lowered them to the floor, pulling her on top of him. He held her tightly at the hip and the shoulder. Part of him was worried about the host and hostess and the other people in the room but another part of him could not stop the crazy thing which had begun. Her fingers opened his shirt to the navel, her tongue burned his neck and his chest; and his hands pushed up her skirt and caressed the inside of her thighs. Then, after a long, high time, while he shook beneath every accelerating tremor of her body, he forced her beneath him and he entered her. For a moment he thought she was going to scream, she was so tight and caught her breath so sharply, and stiffened so. But then she moaned, she moved beneath him. Then, from the center of his rising storm, very slowly and deliberately, he began the slow ride home.

And she carried him, as the sea will carry a boat: with a slow, rocking and rising and falling motion, barely suggestive of the violence of the deep. They murmured and sobbed on this journey, he softly, insistently cursed. Each labored to reach a harbor: there could be no rest until this motion became unbearably accelerated by the power that was rising in them both. Rufus opened his eyes for a moment and watched her face, which was transfigured with agony and gleamed in the darkness like alabaster. Tears hung in the corners of her eyes and the hair at her brow was wet. Her breath came with moaning and short cries, with words he couldn't understand, and in spite of himself he began moving faster and thrusting deeper. He wanted her to remember him the longest day she lived. And, shortly, nothing could have stopped him, not the white God himself nor a lynch mob arriving on wings. Under his breath he cursed the milk-white bitch and groaned and rode his weapon between her thighs. She began to cry. *I told you,* he moaned, *I'd give you something to cry about,* and, at once, he felt himself strangling, about to explode or die. A moan and a curse tore through him while he beat her with all the strength he had and felt the venom shoot out of him, enough for a hundred black-white babies.

He lay on his back, breathing hard. He heard music coming from the room inside, and a whistle on the river.

He was frightened and his throat was dry. The air was chilly where he was wet.

She touched him and he jumped. Then he forced himself to turn to her, looking into her eyes. Her eyes were wet still, deep and dark, her trembling lips curved slightly in a shy, triumphant smile. He pulled her to him, wishing he could rest. He hoped she would say nothing but, "It was so wonderful," she said, and kissed him. And these words, though they caused him to feel no tenderness and did not take away his dull, mysterious dread, began to call desire back again.

He sat up. "You're a funny little cracker," he said. He watched her. "I don't know what you going to say to your husband when you come home with a little black baby."

"I ain't going to be having no more babies," she said, "you ain't got to worry about that." She said nothing more; but she had much more to say. "He beat that out of me, too," she said finally.

He wanted to hear her story. And he wanted to know nothing more about her.

"Let's go inside and wash up," he said.

She put her head against his chest. "I'm afraid to go in there now."

He laughed and stroked her hair. He began to feel affection for her again. "You ain't fixing to stay here all night, are you?"

"What are your friends going to think?"

"Well, one thing, Leona, they ain't going to call the law." He kissed her. "They ain't going to think nothing, honey."

"You coming in with me?"

"Sure, I'm coming in with you." He held her away from him. "All you got to do is sort of straighten your clothes"—he stroked her body, looking into her eyes—"and sort of run your hand through your hair, like this"—and he brushed her hair back from her forehead. She watched him. He heard himself ask, "Do you like me?"

She swallowed. He watched the vein in her neck throb. She seemed very fragile. "Yes," she said. She looked down. "Rufus," she said, "I really do like you. Please don't hurt me."

"Why should I want to hurt you, Leona?" He stroked her neck with one hand, looking at her gravely. "What makes you think I want to hurt you?"

"People *do*," she said, finally, "hurt each other."

"Is somebody been hurting you, Leona?"

She was silent, her face leaning into his palm. "My husband," she said, faintly. "I thought he loved me, but he didn't—oh, I knew he was rough but I didn't think he was *mean*. And he couldn't of loved me because he took away my kid, he's off someplace where I can't never see him." She looked up at Rufus with her eyes full of tears. "He said I wasn't a fit mother because—I—drank too much. I *did* drink too much, it was the only way I could stand living with him. But I would of died for my kid, I wouldn't never of let anything happen to him."

He was silent. Her tears fell on his dark fist. "He's still down there," she said, "my husband, I mean. Him and my mother and my brother is as thick as thieves. They think I ain't never been no good. Well, hell, if people keep telling you you ain't no good"—she tried to laugh—"you bound to turn out pretty bad."

He pushed out of his mind all of the questions he wanted to ask her. It was beginning to be chilly on the balcony; he was hungry and he wanted a drink and he wanted to get home to bed. "Well," he said, at last, "I ain't going to hurt you," and he rose, walking to the edge of the balcony. His shorts were like a rope between his legs, he pulled them up, and felt that he was glued inside them. He zipped up his fly, holding his legs wide apart. The sky had faded down to purple. The stars were gone and the lights on the Jersey shore were out. A coal barge traveled slowly down the river.

"How do I look?" she asked him.

"Fine," he said, and she did. She looked like a tired child. "You want to come down to my place?"

"If you want me to," she said.

"Well, yes, that's what I want." But he wondered why he was holding on to her.

Vivaldo came by late the next afternoon to find Rufus still in bed and Leona in the kitchen making breakfast.

It was Leona who opened the door. And Rufus watched with delight the slow shock on Vivaldo's face as he looked from Leona, muffled in Rufus' bathrobe, to Rufus, sitting up in bed, and naked except for the blankets.

Let the liberal white bastard squirm, he thought.

"Hi, baby," he called, "come on in. You just in time for breakfast."

"I've *had* my breakfast," Vivaldo said, "but you people aren't even decent yet. I'll come back later."

"Shit, man, come on in. That's Leona. Leona, this here's a friend of mine, Vivaldo. For short. His real name is Daniel Vivaldo Moore. He's an Irish wop."

"Rufus is just full of prejudice against everybody," said Leona, and smiled. "Come on in."

Vivaldo closed the door behind him awkwardly and sat down on the edge of the bed. Whenever he was uncomfortable—which was often—his arms and legs seemed to stretch to monstrous proportions and he handled them with bewildered loathing, as though he had been afflicted with them only a few moments before.

"I hope you can eat *something*," Leona said. "There's plenty and it'll be ready in just a second."

"I'll have a cup of coffee with you," Vivaldo said, "unless you happen to have some beer." Then he looked over at Rufus. "I guess it was quite a party."

Rufus grinned. "Not bad, not bad."

Leona opened some beer and poured it into a tumbler

and brought it to Vivaldo. He took it, looking up at her with his quick, gypsy smile, and spilled some on one foot.

"You want some, Rufus?"

"No, honey, not yet. I'll eat first."

Leona walked back into the kitchen.

"Ain't she a splendid specimen of Southern woman-hood?" Rufus asked. "Down yonder, they teach their womenfolks to *serve*."

From the kitchen came Leona's laugh. "They sure don't teach us nothing else."

"Honey, as long as you know how to make a man as happy as you making me, you don't *need* to know nothing else."

Rufus and Vivaldo looked at each other a moment. Then Vivaldo grinned. "How about it, Rufus. You going to get your ass up out of that bed?"

Rufus threw back the covers and jumped out of bed. He raised his arms high and yawned and stretched.

"You're giving quite a show this afternoon," Vivaldo said, and threw him a pair of shorts.

Rufus put on the shorts and an old pair of gray slacks and a faded green sport shirt. "You should have made it to that party," he said, "after all. There was some pot on the scene that wouldn't wait."

"Well. I had my troubles last night."

"You and Jane? As usual?"

"Oh, she got drunk and pulled some shit. You know. She's sick, she can't help it."

"I know *she's* sick. But what's wrong with you?"

"I guess I just like to get beaten over the head." They walked to the table. "This your first time in the Village, Leona?"

"No, I've walked around here some. But you don't really know a place unless you know some of the people."

"You know us now," said Vivaldo, "and between us we must know everybody else. We'll show you around."

Something in the way Vivaldo said this irritated Rufus. His buoyancy evaporated; sour suspicions filled him. He stole a look at Vivaldo, who was sipping his beer and watching Leona with an impenetrable smile—impenetrable exactly because it seemed so open and good-natured. He looked at Leona, who, this afternoon anyway, drowning in his bathrobe, her hair piled on top of her head and her face innocent of make-up, couldn't really be called a pretty girl. Perhaps Vivaldo was contemptuous of her because she was so plain—which meant that Vivaldo was contemptuous of *him*. Or perhaps he was flirting with her because she seemed so simple and available: the proof of her availability being her presence in Rufus' house.

Then Leona looked across the table and smiled at him. His heart and his bowels shook; he remembered their violence and their tenderness together; and he thought,

To hell with Vivaldo. He had something Vivaldo would never be able to touch.

He leaned across the table and kissed her.

"Can I have some more beer?" asked Vivaldo, smiling.

"You know where it is," Rufus said.

Leona took his glass and went to the kitchen. Rufus stuck out his tongue at Vivaldo, who was watching him with a faintly quizzical frown.

Leona returned and set a fresh beer before Vivaldo and said, "You boys finish up now, I'm going to get dressed." She gathered her clothes together and vanished into the bathroom.

There was silence at the table for a moment.

"She going to stay here with you?" Vivaldo asked.

"I don't know yet. Nothing's been decided yet. But I think she wants to—"

"Oh, that's obvious. But isn't this place a little small for two?"

"Maybe we'll find a bigger place. Anyway—you know—I'm not home a hell of a lot."

Vivaldo seemed to consider this. Then, "I hope you know what you're doing, baby. I know it's none of my business, but—"

Rufus looked at him. "Don't you like her?"

"Sure, I like her. She's a sweet girl." He took a swallow of his beer. "The question is—how much do *you* like her?"

"Can't you tell?" And Rufus grinned.

"Well, no, frankly—I can't. I mean, sure you like her. But—oh, I don't know."

There was silence again. Vivaldo dropped his eyes.

"There's nothing to worry about," said Rufus. "I'm a big boy, you know."

Vivaldo raised his eyes and said, "It's a pretty big world, too, baby. I hope you've thought of that."

"I've thought of that."

"Trouble is, I feel too paternal towards you, you son of a bitch."

"That's the trouble with all you white bastards."

They encountered the big world when they went out into the Sunday streets. It stared unsympathetically out at them from the eyes of the passing people; and Rufus realized that he had not thought at all about this world and its power to hate and destroy. He had not thought at all about his future with Leona, for the reason that he had never considered that they had one. Yet, here she was, clearly intending to stay if he would have her. But the price was high: trouble with the landlord, with the neighbors, with all the adolescents in the Village and all those who descended during the weekends. And his family would have a fit. It didn't matter so very much about his father and mother—their fit, having lasted a lifetime, was now not much more than reflex action. But he knew

that Ida would instantly hate Leona. She had always
expected a great deal from Rufus, and she was very race-
conscious. She would say, You'd never even have looked
at that girl, Rufus, if she'd been black. But you'll pick up
any white trash just because she's white. What's the matter—
you ashamed of being black?

Then, for the first time in his life, he wondered about
that—or, rather, the question bumped against his mind for
an instant and then speedily, apologetically, withdrew. He
looked sideways at Leona. Now she was quite pretty. She
had plaited her hair and pinned the braids up, so that she
looked very old-fashioned and much younger than her age.

A young couple came toward them, carrying the Sunday papers. Rufus watched the eyes of the man as the
man looked at Leona; and then both the man and the
woman looked swiftly from Vivaldo to Rufus as though
to decide which of the two was her lover. And, since this
was the Village—the place of liberation—Rufus guessed,
from the swift, nearly sheepish glance the man gave them
as they passed, that he had decided that Rufus and Leona
formed the couple. The face of his wife, however, simply
closed tight, like a gate.

They reached the park. Old, slatternly women from the
slums and from the East Side sat on benches, usually alone,
sometimes sitting with gray-haired, matchstick men. Ladies
from the big apartment buildings on Fifth Avenue, vaguely
and desperately elegant, were also in the park, walking

their dogs; and Negro nursemaids, turning a stony face on the grown-up world, crooned anxiously into baby carriages. The Italian laborers and small-business men strolled with their families or sat beneath the trees, talking to each other; some played chess or read *L'Espresso*. The other Villagers sat on benches, reading—Kierkegaard was the name shouting from the paper-covered volume held by a short-cropped girl in blue jeans—or talking distractedly of abstract matters, or gossiping or laughing; or sitting still, either with an immense, invisible effort which all but shattered the benches and the trees, or else with a limpness which indicated that they would never move again.

Rufus and Vivaldo—but especially Vivaldo—had known or been intimate with many of these people, so long ago, it now seemed, that it might have occurred in another life. There was something frightening about the aspect of old friends, old lovers, who had, mysteriously, come to nothing. It argued the presence of some cancer which had been operating in them, invisibly, all along and which might, now, be operating in oneself. Many people had vanished, of course, had returned to the havens from which they had fled. But many others were still visible, had turned into lushes or junkies or had embarked on a nerve-rattling pursuit of the perfect psychiatrist; were vindictively married and progenitive and fat; were dreaming the same dreams they had dreamed ten years before, clothed these in the same arguments, quoted the same masters; and dispensed, as they hideously imagined, the same charm they had possessed before their teeth began to fail and their hair began to fall. They were more hostile now than they had been, this was the loud, inescapable change in their tone and the only vitality left in their eyes.

Then Vivaldo was stopped on the path by a large, good-natured girl, who was not sober. Rufus and Leona paused, waiting for him.

"Your friend's real nice," said Leona. "He's real natural. I feel like we known each other for years."

Without Vivaldo, there was a difference in the eyes which watched them. Villagers, both bound and free, looked them over as though where they stood were an auction block or a stud farm. The pale spring sun seemed very hot on the back of his neck and on his forehead. Leona gleamed before him and seemed to be oblivious of everything and everyone but him. And if there had been any doubt concerning their relationship, her eyes were enough to dispel it. Then he thought, If she could take it so calmly, if she noticed nothing, what was the matter with him? Maybe he was making it all up, maybe nobody gave a damn. Then he raised his eyes and met the eyes of an Italian adolescent. The boy was splashed by the sun falling through the trees. The boy looked at him with hatred; his glance flicked over Leona as though she were a whore; he dropped his eyes slowly and swaggered on—having registered his protest, his backside seemed to snarl, having made his point.

"Cock sucker," Rufus muttered.

Then Leona surprised him. "You talking about that boy? He's just bored and lonely, don't know no better. You could probably make friends with him real easy if you tried."

He laughed.

"Well, that's what's the matter with most people," Leona insisted, plaintively, "ain't got nobody to be with. That's what makes them so evil. I'm telling you, boy, I know."

"Don't call me *boy*," he said.

"Well," she said, looking startled, "I didn't mean nothing by it, honey." She took his arm and they turned to look for Vivaldo. The large girl had him by the collar and he was struggling to get away, and laughing.

"That Vivaldo," said Rufus, amused, "he has more trouble with women."

"He's sure enjoying it," Leona said. "Look like she's enjoying it, too."

For now the large girl had let him go and seemed about to collapse on the path with laughter. People, with a tolerant smile, looked up from the benches or the grass or their books, recognizing two Village characters.

Then Rufus resented all of them. He wondered if he and Leona would dare to make such a scene in public, if such a day could ever come for them. No one dared to look at Vivaldo, out with any girl whatever, the way they looked at Rufus now; nor would they ever look at the girl the way they looked at Leona. The lowest whore in Manhattan would be protected as long as she had Vivaldo on her arm. This was because Vivaldo was white.

He remembered a rainy night last winter, when he had just come in from a gig in Boston, and he and Vivaldo had gone out with Jane. He had never really understood what Vivaldo saw in Jane, who was too old for him, and combative and dirty; her gray hair was never combed, her sweaters, of which she seemed to possess thousands, were all equally raveled and shapeless; and her blue jeans were baggy and covered with paint. "She dresses like a goddamn bull dagger," Rufus had told Vivaldo once, and then laughed at Vivaldo's horrified expression. His face had puckered as though someone had just cracked a rotten egg. But he had never really hated Jane until this rainy night.

It had been a terrible night, with rain pouring down like great tin buckets, filling the air with a roaring, whining clatter, and making lights and streets and buildings as fluid as itself. It battered and streamed against the windows of the fetid, poor-man's bar Jane had brought them to, a bar where they knew no one. It was filled with shapeless, filthy women with whom Jane drank, apparently, sometimes, during the day; and pale, untidy, sullen men, who worked on the docks, and resented seeing him there. He wanted to go, but he was trying to wait for the rain to let up a little. He was bored speechless with Jane's chatter about her paintings, and he was ashamed of Vivaldo for putting up with it. How had the fight begun? He had always blamed it on Jane. Finally, in order not to go to sleep, he had begun to tease Jane a little; but this teasing revealed, of course, how he really felt about her, and she was not slow to realize it. Vivaldo watched them with a faint, wary smile. He, too, was bored, and found Jane's pretensions intolerable.

"Anyway," Jane said, "you aren't an artist and so I don't see how you can possibly judge the work I do—"

"Oh, stop it," said Vivaldo. "Do you know how silly you sound? You mean you just paint for this half-assed gang of painters down here?"

"Oh, let her swing, man," Rufus said, beginning to enjoy himself. He leaned forward, grinning at Jane in a way at once lewd and sardonic. "This chick's too deep for us, man, we can't dig that shit she's putting down."

"You're the snobs," she said, "not I. I bet you I've reached more people, honest, hard-working, ignorant people, right here in this bar, than either of you ever reach. Those people you hang out with are *dead,* man—at least, these people are *alive.*"

Rufus laughed. "I thought it smelled funny in here. So that's it. Shit. It's life, huh?" And he laughed again.

But he was also aware that they were beginning to attract attention, and he glanced at the windows where the rain streamed down, saying to himself, Okay, Rufus, behave yourself. And he leaned back in the booth, where he sat facing Jane and Vivaldo.

He had reached her, and she struck back with the only weapon she had, a shapeless instrument which might once have been fury. "It doesn't smell any worse in here than it does where you come from, baby."

Vivaldo and Rufus looked at each other. Vivaldo's lips turned white. He said, "You say another word, baby, and I'm going to knock your teeth, both of them, right down your throat."

This profoundly delighted her. She became Bette Davis at once, and shouted at the top of her voice, "Are you threatening me?"

Everyone turned to look at them.

"Oh, shit," said Rufus, "let's go."

"Yes," said Vivaldo, "let's get out of here." He looked at Jane. "Move. You filthy bitch."

And now she was contrite. She leaned forward and grabbed Rufus' hand. "I didn't mean it the way it sounded." He tried to pull his hand away; she held on. He relaxed, not wanting to seem to struggle with her. Now she was being Joan Fontaine. "Please, you *must* believe me, Rufus!"

"I believe you," he said, and rose; to find a heavy Irishman standing in his way. They stared at each other for a moment and then the man spit in his face. He heard Jane scream, but he was already far away. He struck, or thought he struck; a fist slammed into his face and something hit him at the back of the head. The world, the air, went red and black, then roared in at him with faces and fists. The small of his back slammed against something cold, hard, and straight; he supposed it was the end of the bar, and he wondered how he had got there. From far away, he saw a barstool poised above Vivaldo's head, and he heard Jane screaming, keening like all of Ireland. He had not known there were so many men in the bar. He struck a face, he felt bone beneath the bone of his fist, and weak green eyes, glaring into his like headlights at the moment of collision, shuttered in distress. Someone had reached him in the belly, someone else in the head. He was being spun about and he could no longer strike, he could only defend. He kept his head down, bobbing and shifting, pushed and pulled, and he crouched, trying to protect his private parts. He heard the crash of glass. For an instant he saw Vivaldo, at the far end of the bar, blood streaming down from his nose and his forehead, surrounded by three or four men, and he saw the back of a hand send Jane spinning half across the room. Her face was white and terrified. *Good,* he thought, and felt himself in the air, going over the bar. Glass crashed again, and wood was splintered. There was a foot on his shoulder and a foot on one ankle. He pressed his buttocks against the floor and drew his free leg in as far as he could; and with one arm he tried to hold back the fist which crashed down again and again into his face. Far behind the fist was the face of the Irishman, with the green eyes ablaze. Then he saw nothing, heard nothing, felt nothing. Then he heard running feet. He was on his back behind the bar. There was no one near him. He pulled himself up and half-crawled out. The bartender was at the door, shooing his customers out; an old woman sat at the bar, tranquilly sipping gin; Vivaldo lay on his face in a pool of blood. Jane stood helplessly over him. And the sound of the rain came back.

"I think he's dead," Jane said.

He looked at her, hating her with all his heart. He said, "I wish to God it was you, you cunt." She began to cry.

He leaned down and helped Vivaldo to rise. Half-leaning on, half-supporting each other, they made it to the door. Jane came behind them. "Let me help you."

Vivaldo stopped and tried to straighten. They leaned, half-in, half-out of the door. The bartender watched them. Vivaldo looked at the bartender, then at Jane. He and Rufus stumbled together into the blinding rain.

"Let me *help* you," Jane cried again. But she stopped in the doorway long enough to say to the bartender, whose face held no expression whatever, "You're going to hear about this, believe me. I'm going to close this bar and have your job, if it's the last thing I ever do." Then she ran into the rain, and tried to help Rufus support Vivaldo.

Vivaldo pulled away from her touch, and slipped and almost fell. "Get away from me. Get away from me. You've been enough help for one night."

"You've got to get in somewhere!" Jane cried.

"Don't you *worry* about it. Don't worry about it. Drop dead, get lost, go fuck yourself. We're going to the hospital."

Rufus looked into Vivaldo's face and became frightened. Both his eyes were closing and the blood poured down from some wound in his scalp. And he was crying.

"What a way to talk to my buddy, man," he said, over and over. "Wow! What a way to talk to my *buddy*!"

"Let's go to her place," Rufus whispered. "It's closer." Vivaldo did not seem to hear him. "Come on, baby, let's go on over to Jane's, it don't matter."

He was afraid that Vivaldo had been badly hurt, and he knew what would happen at the hospital if two fays and a spade came bleeding in. For the doctors and nurses were, first of all, upright, clean-living white citizens. And he was not really afraid for himself, but for Vivaldo, who knew so little about his countrymen.

So, slipping and sliding, with Jane now circling helplessly around them and now leading the way, like a big-assed Joan of Arc, they reached Jane's pad. He carried Vivaldo into the bathroom and sat him down. He looked in the mirror. His face looked like jam, but the scars would probably heal, and only one eye was closed; but when he began washing Vivaldo, he found a great gash in his skull, and this frightened him.

"Man," he whispered, "you got to go to the hospital."

"That's what I said. All right. Let's go."

And he tried to rise.

"No, man. Listen. If I go with you, it's going to be a whole lot of who shot John because I'm black and you're white. You dig? I'm telling it to you like it is."

Vivaldo said, "I really don't want to hear all that shit, Rufus."

"Well, it's true, whether you want to hear it or not. Jane's got to take you to the hospital, I can't come with you." Vivaldo's eyes were closed and his face was white. "Vivaldo?"

He opened his eyes. "Are you mad at me, Rufus?"

"Shit, no, baby, why should I be mad with you?" But he knew what was bothering Vivaldo. He leaned down and whispered, "Don't you worry, baby, everything's cool. I know you're my friend."

"I love you, you shithead, I really do."

"I love you, too. Now, get on to that hospital, I don't want you to drop dead in this phony white chick's bath-room. I'll wait here for you. I'll be all right." Then he walked quickly out of the bathroom. He said to Jane, "Take him to the hospital, he's hurt worse than I am. I'll wait here."

She had the sense, then, to say nothing. Vivaldo remained in the hospital for ten days and had three stitches taken in his scalp. In the morning Rufus went uptown to see a doctor and stayed in bed for a week. He and Vivaldo never spoke of this night, and though he knew that Vivaldo had finally begun seeing her again, they never spoke of Jane. But from that time on, Rufus had depended on and trusted Vivaldo—depended on him even now, as he bitterly watched him horsing around with the large girl on the path. He did not know why this was so; he scarcely knew that it was so. Vivaldo was unlike everyone else that he knew in that they, all the others, could only astonish him by kindness or fidelity; it was only Vivaldo who had the power to astonish him by treachery. Even his affair with Jane was evidence in his favor, for if he were really likely to betray his friend for a woman, as most white men seemed to do, especially if the friend were black, then he would have found himself a smoother chick, with the manners of a lady and the soul of a whore. But Jane seemed to be exactly what she was, a monstrous slut, and she thus, without knowing it, kept Rufus and Vivaldo equal to one another.

At last Vivaldo was free and hurried toward them on the path still grinning, and now waving to someone behind them.

"Look," he cried, "there's Cass!"

Rufus turned and there she was, sitting alone on the rim of the circle, frail and fair. For him, she was thoroughly mysterious. He could never quite place her in the white world to which she seemed to belong. She came from New England, of plain old American stock—so she put it; she was very fond of remembering that one of her ancestors had been burned as a witch. She had married Richard, who was Polish, and they had two children. Richard had been Vivaldo's English instructor in high school, years ago. They had known him as a brat, they said—not that he had changed much; they were his oldest friends.

With Leona between them, Rufus and Vivaldo crossed the road.

Cass looked up at them with that smile which was at once chilling and warm. It was warm because it was affectionate; it chilled Rufus because it was amused. "Well, I'm not sure I'm speaking to either of you. You've been neglecting us shamefully. Richard has crossed you *off* his list." She looked at Leona and smiled. "I'm Cass Silenski."

"This is Leona," Rufus said, putting one hand on Leona's shoulder.

Cass looked more amused than ever, and at the same time more affectionate. "I'm very happy to meet you."

"I'm glad to meet *you*," said Leona.

They sat down on the stone rim of the fountain, in the center of which a little water played, enough for small children to wade in.

"Give an account of yourselves," Cass said. "*Why* haven't you come to see us?"

"Oh," said Vivaldo, "I've been busy. I've been working on my novel."

"He's been working on a novel," said Cass to Leona,

"ever since we've known him. Then he was seventeen and now he's nearly thirty."

"That's unkind," said Vivaldo, looking amused at the same time that he looked ashamed and annoyed.

"Well, Richard was working on one, too. Then he was twenty-five and now he's close to forty. So—" She considered Vivaldo a moment. "Only, he's had a brand-new inspiration and he's been working on it like a madman. I think that's one of the reasons he's been rather hoping you'd come by—he may have wanted to discuss it with you."

"What is this new inspiration?" Vivaldo asked. "Offhand, it sounds unfair."

"Ah!"—she shrugged merrily, and took a deep drag on her cigarette—"I wasn't consulted, and I'm kept in the dark. You know Richard. He gets up at some predawn hour and goes straight to his study and stays there until it's time to go to work; comes home, goes straight to his study and stays there until it's time to go to bed. I hardly ever see him. The children no longer have a father, I no longer have a husband." She laughed. "He did manage to grunt something the other morning about its going very well."

"It certainly *sounds* as though it's going well." Vivaldo looked at Cass enviously. "And you say it's new?—it's not the same novel he was working on before?"

"I gather not. But I really know nothing about it." She dragged on her cigarette again, crushed it under her heel, immediately began searching in her bag for another.

"Well, I'll certainly have to come by and check on all this for myself," said Vivaldo. "At this rate, he'll be famous before I am."

"Oh, I've always known that," said Cass, and lit another cigarette.

Rufus watched the pigeons strutting along the walks and the gangs of adolescents roaming up and down. He wanted to get away from this place and this danger. Leona put her hand on his. He grabbed one of her fingers and held it.

Cass turned to Rufus. "Now, *you* haven't been working on a novel, why haven't *you* come by?"

"I've been working uptown. *You* promised to come and hear *me.* Remember?"

"We've been terribly broke, Rufus—"

"When I'm working in a joint, you haven't got to worry about being broke, I told you that before."

"He's a great musician," Leona said. "I heard him for the first time last night."

Rufus looked annoyed. "That gig ended last night. I ain't got nothing to do for awhile except take care of my old lady." And he laughed.

Cass and Leona looked briefly at each other and smiled.

"How long have you been up here, Leona?" Cass asked.

"Oh, just a little over a month."

"Do you like it?"

"Oh, I love it. It's just as different as night from day, I can't tell you."

Cass looked briefly at Rufus. "That's wonderful," she said, gravely. "I'm very glad for you."

"Yes, I can feel that," said Leona. "You seem to be a very nice woman."

"Thank you," said Cass, and blushed.

"*How*'re you going to take care of your old lady," Vivaldo asked, "if you're not working?"

"Oh, I've got a couple of record dates coming up; don't you worry about old Rufus."

Vivaldo sighed. "I'm worried about *me*. I'm in the wrong profession—or, rather, I'm not. *In* it, I mean. Nobody wants to hear my story."

Rufus looked at him. "Don't let me start talking to you about *my* profession."

"Things are tough all over," said Vivaldo.

Rufus looked out over the sun-filled park.

"Nobody ever has to take up a collection to bury managers or agents," Rufus said. "But they sweeping musicians up off the streets every day."

"Never mind," said Leona, gently, "they ain't never going to sweep you up off the streets."

She put her hand on his head and stroked it. He reached up and took her hand away.

There was a silence. Then Cass rose. "I hate to break this up, but I must go home. One of my neighbors took the kids to the zoo, but they're probably getting back by now. I'd better rescue Richard."

"How *are* your kids, Cass?" Rufus asked.

"Much *you* care. It would serve you right if they'd forgotten all about you. They're fine. They've got much more energy than their parents."

Vivaldo said, "I'm going to walk Cass home. What do you think you'll be doing later?"

He felt a dull fear and a dull resentment, almost as though Vivaldo were deserting him. "Oh, I don't know. I guess we'll go along home—"

"I got to go uptown later, Rufus," said Leona. "I ain't got nothing to go to work in tomorrow."

Cass held out her hand to Leona. "It was nice meeting you. Make Rufus bring you by to see us one day."

"Well, it was sure nice meeting you. I been meeting some real nice people lately."

"Next time," said Cass, "we'll go off and have a drink by ourselves someplace, without all these *men*."

They laughed together. "I *really* would like that."

"Suppose I pick you up at Benno's," Rufus said to Vivaldo, "around ten-thirty?"

"Good enough. Maybe we'll go across town and pick up on some jazz?"

"Good."

"So long, Leona. Glad to have met you."

"Me, too. Be seeing you real soon."

"Give my regards," said Rufus, "to Richard and the kids, and tell them I'm coming by."

"I'll do that. Make sure you *do* come by, we'd dearly love to see you."

Cass and Vivaldo started slowly in the direction of the arch. The bright-red, setting sun burned their silhouettes against the air and crowned the dark head and the golden one. Rufus and Leona stood and watched them; when they were under the arch, they turned and waved.

"We better be making tracks," said Rufus.

"I guess so." They started back through the park. "You got some real nice friends, Rufus. You're lucky. They're real fond of you. They think you're somebody."

"You think they do?"

"I know they do. I can tell by the way they talk to you, the way they treat you."

"I guess they *are* pretty nice," he said, "at that."

She laughed. "*You're* a funny boy"—she corrected herself—"a funny *person*. You act like you don't know who you are."

"I know who I am, all right," he said, aware of the eyes that watched them pass, the nearly inaudible murmur that came from the benches or the trees. He squeezed her thin hand between his elbow and his side. "I'm your boy. You know what that means?"

"What does it mean?"

"It means you've got to be good to me."

"Well, Rufus, I sure am going to try."

Writing *The Amen Corner* I remember as a desperate and even rather irresponsible act—it was certainly considered irresponsible by my agent at that time. She did not wish to discourage me, but it was her duty to let me know that the American theatre was not exactly clamoring for plays on obscure aspects of Negro life, especially one written by a virtually unknown author whose principal effort until that time had been one novel. She may sincerely have believed that I had gotten my signals mixed and earnestly explained to me that, with one novel under my belt, it was the *magazine* world that was open to me, *not* the world of the theatre; I sensibly ought to be pursuing the avenue that was open, especially since I had no money at all. I couldn't explain to her or to myself why I wasted so much time on a play. I knew, for one thing, that very few novelists are able to write plays and I really had no reason to suppose that I could be an exception to this age-old, iron rule. I was perfectly aware that it would probably never be produced, and, furthermore, I didn't even have any ambition to conquer the theatre. To this last point we shall return, for I was being very dishonest, or perhaps merely very cunning, with myself concerning the extent of my ambition.

I had written one novel, *Go Tell It on the Mountain,* and it had taken me a long time, nearly ten years, to do it. Those ten years had taken me from Harlem, through the horrors of being a civilian employee (unskilled) of the army in New Jersey, to being an unskilled employee, period. There is no point in trying to describe the sheer physical terror which was my life in those days, for I was simply grotesquely out of my setting and everyone around me knew it, and made me pay for it. I say "everyone" for the sake of convenience, for there were, indeed, exceptions, thank God, and these exceptions helped to save my life and also taught me what I then most bitterly needed to know— *i.e.,* that love and compassion, which always arrive in such unexpected packages, have nothing to do with the color of anybody's skin. For I was simply another black boy; there were millions like me at the mercy of the labor market, to say nothing of the labor unions, and it was very clear to me that in the jungle in which I found myself I had no future at all: my going under was simply a matter of time.

But, on the other hand, I had a family—a mother and eight younger brothers and sisters—and something in me knew that if I were to betray them and the love we bore each other, I would be destroying myself. Yet there was no possibility that I would ever be of any use to them, or anyone else, if I continued my life in factories. I was, unfortunately, not equipped for anything but hard labor. No one would ever look at me and offer me anything more than a menial job, and yet people very frequently hesitated to offer me the only jobs open to me because they obscurely felt that I was unreliable, probably inflammatory, and far more trouble than I could possibly be worth. Well, to tell the truth, I can't say very much about those years; I suppose I've blotted it out. What I did, finally, was allow myself to drop to the very bottom of the labor market, became a busboy and short-order cook in places like Riker's—and wrote all the time. And when I was twenty-four, I took the last of a Rosenwald Fellowship grant and bought a plane ticket to Paris. I bought a plane ticket because I was afraid I would lose my nerve if I waited for a boat. I got to Paris with forty dollars and no French. I slid downhill with impressive speed, which wasn't difficult considering the slightness of my eminence, ended up, successively, in one French hospital and one French jail, and then took stock. I was twenty-five and didn't have much to show for it. I started again. By 1952, I finished *Mountain,* borrowed money from Marlon

Brando, one of the great and beautiful exceptions referred to above, and came home to try to sell it. I came home in the summertime, and it may have been the emotional climate and the events of that summer which caused me to write *The Amen Corner.*

I had been away for four years—four very crucial and definitive years. I myself have described my exile as a self-exile, but it was really far more complex and bitter than that. No one really wishes to leave his homeland. I left because I was driven out, because my homeland would not allow me to grow in the only direction in which I could grow. This is but another way of saying that all my countrymen had been able to offer me during the twenty-four years that I tried to live here was death—and death, moreover, on their terms. I had been lucky enough to defeat their intention, and, physically, I had escaped. But I had not escaped myself, I had not escaped my antecedents, not even France could compensate for some of the things I knew and felt that I was losing; no French-man or Frenchwoman could meet me with the speed and fire of some black boys and girls whom I remembered and whom I missed; they did not know enough about me to be able to correct me. It is true that they met me with something else—themselves, in fact—and taught me things I did not know (how to take a deep breath, for example) and corrected me in unexpected and rather painful ways. But it was not really my home. I might live there forever and it would never be my home. No matter how immensely I might become reconciled to my condition, it was, nevertheless, the specialness of my condition which had driven me to France. And I had to know this; I could not, on pain of death, forget it—or, rather, to forget it would mean that my high pretensions were nothing but a fraud, that the anguish of my forebears meant nothing to me, and that I had never really intended to become a writer but had only been trying to be safe.

In New York that summer all this became very vivid to me—as vivid as a wound; and it was I, it seemed to me, who had become a kind of ambulating anguish. Not only had New York not changed—as far as I could see, it had become worse; and my hope of ever being able to live in New York diminished with every hour. And this distress was inconceivably aggravated by the one circumstance which would have seemed to be able to alleviate it: the fact that I was a young writer, with a small reputation and a possible future, whose first novel was about to be published. But, to tell the truth, I was really a young *Negro* writer, and the world into which I was moving quite helplessly, and quite without malice, had its own expectations of me, expectations which I was determined to defeat.

The editor assigned to me and my book asked me, when I entered his office for the first time and after the book had been accepted, "What about all that come-to-Jesus stuff? Don't you think you ought to take it out?" *Go*

Tell It on the Mountain is the study of a Negro evangelist
and his family. They do, indeed, talk in a "come-to-Jesus"
idiom, but to "take it out" could only mean that my editor was suggesting that I burn the book. I gagged, literally,
and began to sweat, ran to the water cooler, tried to pull
myself together, and returned to the office to explain the
intention of my novel. I learned a great deal that afternoon; learned, to put it far too briefly, what I was up
against; took the check and went back to Paris.

I went back to Paris, as I then thought, for good, and
my reasons this time seemed very different from the reasons which had driven me there in the first place. My
original reasons were that I had been forced, most reluc-
tantly, to recognize that thought was also action; what
one saw, the point of view from which one viewed the
world, dictated what one did; and this meant, in my situation, that I was in danger, most literally, of *thinking*
myself out of existence. I was not expected to know the
things I knew, or to say the things I said, to make the kind
of jokes I made, or to do the things I did. I knew that I
was a black street-boy, and that knowledge was all I had. I
could not delude myself about it. I did not even have the
rather deadly temptations of being good-looking, for I
knew that I was not good-looking. All I had, in a word,
was me, and I was forced to insist on this *me* with all the
energy I had. Naturally, I got my head broken, naturally
people laughed when I said I was going to be a writer,

and naturally, since I wanted to live, I finally split the scene. But when I came back to sell my first novel, I realized that I was being corraled into another trap: now I was a writer, a *Negro* writer, and I was expected to write diminishing versions of *Go Tell It on the Mountain* forever.

Which I refused to do. I had not, after all, paid all those dues for that. I had no idea whether or not I could write a play, but I was absolutely determined that I would not, not at that moment in my career, not at that moment in my life, attempt another novel. I did not trust myself to do it. I was really terrified that I would, without even knowing that I was doing it, try to repeat my first success and begin to imitate myself. I knew that I had more to say and much, much more to discover than I had been able to indicate in *Mountain*. Poverty is not a crime in Paris; it does not mean that you are a worthless person; and so I returned and began what I told myself was a "writing exercise": by which I meant I'm still a young man, my family now knows that I really am a writer—that was very important to me—let us now see if I am equipped to go the distance, and let's try something we've never tried before. The first line written in *The Amen Corner* is now Margaret's line in the Third Act: "It's a awful thing to think about, the way love never dies!" That line, of course, says a great deal about me—the play says a great deal about me—but I was thinking not only, not merely, about the terrifying desolation of my private life but about the great burdens carried by my father. I was old enough by now, at last, to recognize the nature of the dues he had paid, old enough to wonder if I could possibly have paid them, old enough, at last, at last, to know that I had loved him and had wanted him to love me. I could see that the nature of the battle we had fought had been dictated by the fact that our temperaments were so fatally the same: neither of us could bend. And when I began to think about what had happened to him, I began to see why he was so terrified of what was surely going to happen to me.

The Amen Corner comes somewhere out of that. For to think about my father meant that I had also to think about my mother and the stratagems she was forced to use to save her children from the destruction awaiting them just outside her door. It is because I know what Sister Margaret goes through, and what her male child is menaced by, that I become so unmanageable when people ask me to confirm their hope that there has been *progress*—what a word!—in white-black relations. There has certainly not been enough progress to solve Sister Margaret's dilemma: how to treat her husband and her son as men and at the same time to protect them from the bloody consequences of trying to be a man in this society. No one yet knows, or is in the least prepared to speculate on, how high a bill we will yet have to pay for what we have done to Negro men and women. She is in the church

because her society has left her no other place to go. Her
sense of reality is dictated by the society's assumption,
which also becomes her own, of her inferiority. Her need
for human affirmation, and also for vengeance, expresses
itself in her merciless piety; and her love, which is real but
which is also at the mercy of her genuine and absolutely
justifiable terror, turns her into a tyrannical matriarch. In
all of this, of course, she loses her old self—the fiery, fast-
talking little black woman whom Luke loved. Her triumph, which is also, if I may say so, the historical triumph
of the Negro people in this country, is that she sees this
finally and accepts it, and, although she has lost everything,
also gains the keys to the kingdom. The kingdom is love,
and love is selfless, although only the self can lead one there.
She gains herself.

One last thing: concerning my theatrical ambitions,
and my cunning or dishonesty—I was armed, I knew, in
attempting to write the play, by the fact that I was born in
the church. I knew that out of the ritual of the church,
historically speaking, comes the act of the theatre, the
communion which is the theatre. And I knew that what I
wanted to do in the theatre was to re-create moments I
remembered as a boy preacher, to involve the people,
even against their will, to shake them up, and, hopefully,
to change them. I knew that an unknown black writer
could not possibly hope to achieve this forum. I did not
want to enter the theatre on the theatre's terms, but on

mine. And so I waited. And the fact that *The Amen Corner* took ten years to reach the professional stage says a great deal more about the American theatre than it says about this author. The American Negro really is a part of this country, and on the day we face this fact, and not before that day, we will become a nation and possibly a great one.

James Baldwin

from THE AMEN CORNER

Music is heard offstage, a slow, quiet sound.

Early the following morning. A bright quiet day. Except for LUKE, *the stage is empty. His room is dark. He is sleeping.*

The light comes up very slowly in the church. After a moment, MRS. JACKSON *enters. She is wearing a house dress and slippers. She puts her hands to her face, moaning slightly, then falls heavily before the altar.*

MARGARET *enters through* LUKE*'s bedroom. She pauses a moment at the foot of* LUKE*'s bed, then enters the kitchen, then slowly mounts to the church.*

As she enters, MRS. JACKSON *stirs. They stare at each other for a moment.*

MRS. JACKSON *is weeping.*

MRS. JACKSON: Sister Margaret, you's a woman of the Lord—you say you in communion with the Lord. Why

He take my baby from me? Tell me why He do it? Why He make my baby suffer so? Tell me why He do it!

MARGARET: Sister—we got to trust God—somehow. We got to bow our heads.

MRS. JACKSON: My head is bowed. My head been bowed since I been born. His daddy's head is bowed. The Lord ain't got no right to make a baby suffer so, just to make me bow my head!

MARGARET: Be careful what you say, daughter. Be careful what you say. We can't penetrate the mysteries of the Lord's will.

MRS. JACKSON (*Moves away*): Why I got to be careful what I say? You think the Lord going to do me something else? I ain't got to be careful what I say no more. I sit on the bench in the hospital all night long, me and my husband, and we waited and we prayed and we wept. I said, Lord, if you spare my baby, I won't never take another drink, I won't do nothing, nothing to displease you, if you only give me back my baby, safe and well. He was such a nice baby and just like his daddy, he liked to laugh already. But I ain't going to have no more. Such a nice baby, I don't see why he had to get all twisted and curled up with pain and scream his little head off. And couldn't nobody help him. He hadn't never done nothing to nobody. Ain't nobody never done nothing bad enough to suffer like that baby suffered.

MARGARET: Daughter, pray with me. Come, pray with me.

MRS. JACKSON: I been trying to pray. Everytime I kneel down, I see my baby again—and—I can't pray. I can't get it out of my head, it ain't right, even if He's God, it ain't right.

MARGARET: Sister—once I lost a baby, too. I know what that emptiness feel like, I declare to my Saviour I do. That was when I come to the Lord. I wouldn't come before. Maybe the Lord is working with you now. Open your heart and listen. Maybe, out of all this sorrow, He's calling you to do His work.

MRS. JACKSON: I ain't like you, Sister Margaret. I don't want all this, all these people looking to me. I'm just a young woman, I just want my man and my home and my children.

MARGARET: But that's all I wanted. That's what I wanted! Sometimes—what we want—and what we ought to have—ain't the same. Sometime, the Lord, He take away what we want and give us what we need.

MRS. JACKSON: And do I need—that man sitting home with a busted heart? Do I need—two children in the graveyard?

MARGARET: I don't know, I ain't the Lord, I don't know what you need. You need to pray.

MRS. JACKSON: No, I'm going home to my husband. He be getting worried. He don't know where I am.

(She starts out.)

MARGARET: Sister Jackson! *(MRS. JACKSON turns.)* Why did

you say you ain't going to have no more babies? You still a very young woman.

MRS. JACKSON: I'm scared to go through it again. I can't go through it again.

MARGARET: That ain't right. That ain't right. You ought to have another baby. You ought to have another baby right away. *(A pause)* Honey—is there anything you want me to do for you now, in your time of trouble?

MRS. JACKSON: No, Sister Margaret, ain't nothing you can do.

(She goes. MARGARET *stands alone in the church.)*

MARGARET: Get on home to your husband. Go on home, to your man.

(Downstairs, ODESSA *enters through* LUKE*'s room; pauses briefly at* LUKE*'s bed, enters the kitchen. She goes to the stove, puts a match under the coffeepot.* MARGARET *stares at the altar; starts downstairs.)*

ODESSA: *(Sings, under her breath)*: Some say the rose of Sharon, some say the Prince of Peace. But I call Jesus my rock!

*(*MARGARET *enters.)*

ODESSA: How long you been up, Maggie?

MARGARET: I don't know. Look like I couldn't sleep.

ODESSA: You got a heavy day ahead of you.

MARGARET: I know it. David ain't come in yet?

ODESSA: No, but don't you fret. He's all right. He'll be along. It's just natural for young boys to go a little wild every now and again. Soon this'll all be over, Maggie, and when you look back on it it won't be nothing more than like you had a bad dream.

MARGARET: A bad dream!

ODESSA: They ain't going to turn you out, Maggie. They ain't crazy. They know it take a *long* time before they going to find another pastor of this church like you.

MARGARET: It won't take them so long if Sister Moore have her way. She going to be the next pastor of this church. Lord, you sure can't tell what's going on in a person's heart.

ODESSA: The Bible say the heart is deceitful above all things. And desperately wicked.

MARGARET: Who can know it? I guess whoever wrote that wasn't just thinking about the hearts of other people.

ODESSA: Maggie, you better go on in the front and lie down awhile. You got time. Sunday school ain't even started yet. I'll call you in time for you to get dressed for service.

MARGARET: I reckon I better. *(She starts out, stops.)* They talk about me letting my own house perish in sin. The Word say if you put father or mother or brother or sister or husband—or *anybody*—ahead of Him, He ain't going to have nothing to do with you on the last day.

ODESSA: Yes. The Word do say so.

MARGARET: I married that man when I weren't hardly nothing but a girl. I used to know that man, look like, just inside *out,* sometime I knowed what he was going to do before he knowed it himself. Sometime I could just look up, look up at that face, and just—*know*. Ain't no man never made me laugh the way Luke could. No, nor cry neither. I ain't never held no man until I felt his pain coming into me like little drops of acid. Odessa, I bore that man his only son. Now, you know there's still something left in my heart for that man.

ODESSA: Don't think on it, honey. Don't think on it so. Go on in front and lie down.

MARGARET: Yes. *(She starts out, stops.)* Odessa—you know what amen means?

ODESSA: Amen means—*amen*.

MARGARET: Amen means Thy will be done. Amen means So be it. I been up all morning, praying—and—I couldn't say amen. *(She goes.)*

ODESSA: Lord, have mercy. Have mercy, Lord, this morning. *(Sings, under her breath)* Some say the Rose of Sharon, some say the Prince of Peace. But I call Jesus my rock! *(She goes to the door of* LUKE's *room.* BROTHER *and* SISTER BOXER *and* SISTER MOORE *enter the church. The two women are all in white.)*

Yes, Lord. Every time a woman don't know if she coming or going, every *time* her heart get all swelled up with grief, there's a man sleeping somewhere close by.

*(*SISTER BOXER *crosses the church and comes down the stairs.)*

SISTER BOXER: Praise the Lord, Sister Odessa. You all alone this morning?

ODESSA: I didn't know you folks was upstairs. How long
    you been there?

SISTER BOXER: We just this minute come in.

ODESSA: You all mighty early, seems to me.

SISTER BOXER: Well, Sister Moore, she thought if we got
    here early we might be able to see Sister Margaret
    before anybody else come in.

ODESSA: Sister Margaret ain't ready to see nobody yet.

SISTER BOXER: It almost time for Sunday school.

ODESSA: Sister Boxer, you know right well that Sister
    Margaret don't hardly never come to Sunday school.
    She got to save her strength for the morning service.
    You know that.

SISTER BOXER: Well, Sister Moore thought—maybe *this*
    morning—

ODESSA: Sister Boxer—don't you think enough harm's been
    done with all them terrible things was said last night?

SISTER BOXER: Ain't nobody said nothing last night that
    wasn't the gospel truth.

ODESSA: I done heard enough truth these last couple of
    days to last me the rest of my life.

SISTER BOXER: The truth is a two-edged sword, Sister
    Odessa.

ODESSA: It ain't never going to cut you down. You ain't
    never going to come that close to it.

SISTER BOXER: Well—do Jesus! Soon as something hap-
    pens to that sister of yours you forgets all about your

salvation, don't you? You better ask the Lord to watch your tongue. The tongue is a *unruly* member.

ODESSA: It ain't as unruly as it's going to get. *(A pause)* Sister Boxer, this ain't no way for us to be talking. We used to be *friends.* We used to have right *good* times together. How come we got all this bad feeling all of a sudden? Look like it come out of nowhere, overnight.

SISTER BOXER: I ain't got no bad feeling toward *you,* Sister Odessa.

(After a moment, SISTER BOXER *turns and mounts to the church.* ODESSA *follows.)*

SISTER MOORE: Praise the Lord, Sister Odessa. How you this Lord's day morning?

ODESSA: I'm leaning on the Lord, Sister Moore. How you feeling?

BROTHER BOXER: Praise the Lord, Sister Odessa. I'm mighty glad to hear you say that. We needs the Lord this morning. We needs to hear Him speak peace to our souls.

ODESSA: How come you folks want to see Sister Margaret so early in the morning?

SISTER BOXER: Well, we ain't really got to see Sister Margaret, not now that you're here, Sister Odessa. You is still one of the elders of this church.

SISTER MOORE: We want to do everything we got to do in front, amen. Don't want nobody saying we went around and done it in the dark.

ODESSA: You's doing it in front, all right. You's supposed to
do it in front of the whole congregation this afternoon.

BROTHER BOXER: Well, the Lord's done led us to do a little
different from the way we was going to do last night.

ODESSA: How's that, Brother Boxer? *(A pause)* Well, now,
the way I understood it last *night*—you folks say that
Margaret ain't got no right to call herself a spiritual
leader. *You* folks say that Margaret done let her own
household perish in sin and—you folks say—that all
these things is a sign from the Lord that He ain't
pleased with Margaret and you was going to put all that
in front of this church and the church from Philadelphia and see what *they* thought. Ain't that right?

SISTER BOXER: We done already spoken to the members of
this church. Margaret's as good as read out of this church
already, ain't hardly no need for her to come to service.

SISTER MOORE: I spoke to them myself. I been up since
early this morning, bless the Lord, just ringing door-
bells and stirring up the people against sin.

ODESSA: You must of got up mighty early.

SISTER MOORE: When the Lord's work is to be done, I gets
up out of my bed. God don't love the slothful. And, look
like the more I do, the more He gives me strength to do.

BROTHER BOXER: We thought it might be easier on Sister
Margaret if we done it this way. Ain't no need for folks
to know all of Sister Margaret's personal business. So
we ain't said nothing about Brother Luke. Folks is

bound to try and put two and two together—but *we* ain't said nothing. We ain't said nothing about Brother David. We is just told the congregation that the Lord's done revealed to the elders of this church that Sister Margaret ain't been leading the life of a holy woman, especially a holy woman in *her* position, is supposed to lead. That's all. And we said we weren't sitting in *judgment* on Sister Margaret. We was leaving it up to her conscience, amen, and the Lord.

SISTER BOXER: But we did say—since we're the elders of the church and we got a responsibility to the congregation, too—that the Lord ain't pleased at Margaret sitting in the seat of authority.

SISTER MOORE: It's time for her to come down.

ODESSA: And how did folks take it when you told them all this?

BROTHER BOXER: Well, folks ain't in this church to worship Sister Margaret. They's here to worship the Lord.

ODESSA: Folks thought Margaret was good enough to be their pastor all these years, they ain't going to stop wanting her for pastor overnight.

BROTHER BOXER: She rose overnight. She can fall overnight.

SISTER BOXER: I tell you, Sister Odessa, like the song says: "You may run on a great, long time but great God Almighty going to cut you down." Yes, indeed, He going to let the truth be known one *day*. And on that day, it's just too bad *for* you. Sister Margaret done had a lot of people fooled a long time, but now, bless God forever, the truth is out.

ODESSA: What truth? What is that woman done to make you hate her so? Weren't but only yesterday you was all saying how wonderful she was, and how blessed we was to have her. And now you can't find nothing bad enough to say about her. Don't give me that stuff about her letting her household perish in sin. Ain't a one of you but ain't got a brother or a sister or somebody on the road to hell right now. I want to know what is she *done*? What is she done to you, Sister Moore?

SISTER BOXER: *I* ain't got no brothers or sisters on the road to hell. Only sister I *had* is waiting for me in glory. And every *soul* I come in contact with is saved—except of course for them people I work for. And I got no trombone-playing husband dying in my house and I ain't got no half-grown son out fornicating in the wilderness.

SISTER MOORE: Don't you come up here and act like you thought we was just acting out of spite and meanness. Your sister ain't done nothing to me; she *can't* do nothing to me because the Lord holds me in His hands. All we's trying to do is the Lord's will—you ought to be trying to do it, too. If we want to reign with him in glory, we ain't supposed to put nobody before Him. Amen! We ain't supposed to have no other love but Him.

SISTER BOXER: I looked at that man and I says to myself,

How in the *world* did Sister Margaret ever get herself mixed up with a man like that?

ODESSA: Ain't no mystery how a woman gets mixed up with a man, Sister Boxer, and you sure ought to know that, even if poor Sister Moore here *don't*.

SISTER MOORE: Don't you poor-Sister-Moore *me*. That man put a demon inside your sister and that demon's walking up and down inside her still. You can see it in her eyes, they done got all sleepy with lust.

ODESSA: Sister Moore, I sure would like to know just how come *you* know so much about it.

SISTER BOXER: Sister Odessa, ain't no sense to you trying to put everybody in the wrong because Sister Margaret is falling. That ain't going to raise her back up. It's the Lord's *will* she should come down.

ODESSA: I don't understand how you can take her part against my sister. *You* ought to know how much Sister Margaret's suffered all these years by herself. *You* know it ain't no easy thing for a woman to go it alone. She done spent more'n ten years to build this up for herself and her little boy. How you going to throw her out now? What's she going to do, where's she going to go?

BROTHER BOXER: She didn't worry about Elder King when she took over this church from him.

SISTER MOORE: I think you think I hates your sister because she been married. And I ain't never been married. I ain't questioning the Lord's ways. He done kept me pure to Himself for a purpose, and that purpose is working itself out right here in this room this morning—right here in this room, this upper room. It make your sister look double-minded, I do declare it do, if she done tried, one time, to bring peace to one man, and failed, and then she jump up and think she going to bring peace to a whole lot of people.

ODESSA: Sister Margaret done give good service all those years. She ain't been acting like she was double-minded.

BROTHER BOXER: But I bet you—she is double-minded *now.* (DAVID *enters the apartment. He is suffering from a hangover, is still a little drunk. He goes to the sink and splashes cold water on his face. He moves with both bravado and fear and there is a kind of heart-breaking humor in his actions.*)

SISTER BOXER: Odessa, a church can't have no woman for pastor who done been married once and then decided it didn't suit her and then jump up and run off from her husband and take a seat in the pulpit and act like she ain't no woman no more. That ain't no kind of example to the young. The Word say the marriage bed is holy.

ODESSA: I can't believe—I can't *believe* you really going to do it. We been friends so long. (DAVID *dries his face. He goes to the door of* LUKE*'s room, stands for a moment looking at his father. He turns back into the kitchen. At this moment,* MARGARET *enters, dressed in white. She and* DAVID *stare at each other.*)

SISTER BOXER: You the one I'm sorry for, Sister Odessa.

You done spent your life, look like, protecting that sister of yours. And now you can't protect her no more.

ODESSA: It ain't been me protecting Sister Margaret. It been the Lord. And He ain't yet withdrawed His hand. He ain't never left none of His children alone.

(She starts for the rear door of the church.)

SISTER BOXER: How come you ain't never been married, Sister Odessa?

ODESSA: Suppose we just say, Sister Boxer, that I never had the time.

SISTER BOXER: It might have been better for you if you'd taken the time.

ODESSA: I ain't got no regrets. No, I ain't. I ain't claiming I'm pure, like Sister Moore here. I ain't claiming that the Lord had such special plans for me that I couldn't have nothing to do with men. Brothers and sisters, if you knew just a little bit about folks' lives, what folks go through, and the low, black places they finds their feet—you *would* have a meeting here this afternoon. Maybe I don't know the Lord like you do, but I know something else. I know how men and women can come together and change each other and make each other suffer, and make each other glad. If you putting my sister out of this church, you putting me out, too.

(She goes out through the street door. The church dims out.)

MARGARET: Where you been until this time in the morning, son?

DAVID: I was out visiting some people I know. And it got to be later than I realized and I stayed there overnight.

MARGARET: How come it got to be so late before you realized it?

DAVID: I don't know. We just got to talking.

MARGARET: Talking? *(She moves closer to him)* What was you talking about, son? You stink of whiskey!

(She slaps him. DAVID *sits at the table.)*

DAVID: That ain't going to do no good, Ma.

(She slaps him again. DAVID *slumps on the table, his head in his arms.)*

MARGARET: Is that what I been slaving for all these long, hard years? Is I carried slops and scrubbed floors and ate leftovers and swallowed bitterness by the gallon jugful—for this? So you could walk in here this Lord's-day morning stinking from whiskey and some no-count, dirty, black girl's sweat? Declare, I wish you'd died in my belly, too, if I been slaving all these years for this!

DAVID: Mama. Mama. Please.

MARGARET: Sit up and look at me. Is you too drunk to hold up your head? Or is you too ashamed? Lord knows you ought to be ashamed.

DAVID: Mama, I wouldn't of had this to happen this way for nothing in the world.

MARGARET: Was they holding a pistol to your head last evening? Or did they tie you down and pour the whiskey down your throat?

DAVID: No. No. Didn't nobody have no pistol. Didn't nobody have no rope. Some fellow said, Let's pick up some whiskey. And I said, Sure. And we all put in some money and I went down to the liquor store and bought it. And then we drank it.

(MARGARET *turns away.*)

MARGARET: David, I ain't so old. I know the world is wicked. I know young people have terrible temptations. Did you do it because you was afraid them boys would make fun of you?

DAVID: No.

MARGARET: Was it on account of some girl?

DAVID: No.

MARGARET: Was it—your daddy put you up to it? Was it your daddy made you think it was manly to get drunk?

DAVID: Daddy—I don't think you can blame it on Daddy, Mama.

MARGARET: Why'd you do it, David? When I done tried so hard to raise you right? Why'd you want to hurt me this way?

DAVID: I didn't want to hurt you, Mama. But this day has been coming a long time. Mama, I can't play piano in church no more.

MARGARET: Is it on account of your daddy? Is it your daddy put all this foolishness in your head?

DAVID: Daddy ain't been around for a long time, Mama. I ain't talked to him but one time since he been here.

MARGARET: And that one time—he told you all about the wonderful time he had all them years, blowing out his guts on that trombone.

DAVID: No. That ain't exactly what he said. That ain't exactly what we talked about.

MARGARET: What *did* you talk about?

(A sound of children singing "Jesus Loves Me" comes from the church.)

DAVID: Well—he must have been talking about you. About how he missed you, and all.

MARGARET: Sunday school done started. David, why don't you go upstairs and play for them, just this one last morning?

DAVID: Mama, I told you. I can't play piano in church no more.

MARGARET: David, why don't you feel it no more, what you felt once? Where's it gone? Where's the Holy Ghost gone?

DAVID: I don't know, Mama. It's empty. *(He indicates his chest)* It's empty here.

MARGARET: Can't you pray? Why don't you pray? If you pray, pray hard, He'll come back. The Holy Ghost will come back. He'll come down on heavenly wings, David, and *(She touches his chest)* fill that empty space, He'll start your heart to singing—singing again. He'll fill you, David, with a mighty burning fire and burn *out (She takes his head roughly between her palms)* all that foolishness, all them foolish dreams you carries around up there. Oh, David, David, pray that the Holy Ghost will come back, that the gift of God will come back!

DAVID: Mama, if a person don't feel it, he just don't feel it.

MARGARET: David, I'm older than you. I done been down the line. I know ain't no safety nowhere in this world if you don't stay close to God. What you think the world's got out there for you but a broken heart?

(ODESSA, *unnoticed, enters.*)

ODESSA: You better listen to her, David.

MARGARET: I remember boys like you down home, David, many years ago—fine young men, proud as horses, and I seen what happened to them. I seen them go down, David, until they was among the lowest of the low. There's boys like you down there, today, breaking rock and building roads, they ain't never going to hold up their heads up on this earth no more. There's boys like you all over this city, filling up the gin mills and standing on the corners, running down alleys, tearing themselves to pieces with knives and whiskey and dope and sin! You think I done lived this long and I don't know what's happening? Fine young men and they're lost— they don't know what's happened to their life. Fine young men, and some of them dead and some of them dead while they living. You think I want to see this happen to you? You think I want you one day lying where your daddy lies today?

ODESSA: You better listen to her David. You better listen.

MARGARET: No. He ain't going to listen. Young folks don't
never listen. They just go on, headlong, and they think
ain't nothing ever going to be too big for them. And,
time they find out, it's too late then.

DAVID: And if I listened—what would happen? What do
you think would happen if I listened? You want me to
stay here, getting older, getting sicker—hating you? You
think I want to hate you, Mama? You think it don't tear
me to pieces to have to lie to you all the time. Yes,
because I been lying to you, Mama, for a long time now!
I don't want to tell no more lies. I don't want to keep on
feeling so bad inside that I have to go running down
them alleys you was talking about—that alley right outside this door!—to find something to help me hide—
to hide—from what I'm feeling. Mama, I want to be a
man. It's time you let me be a man. You got to let me go.
(A pause.)

If I stayed here—I'd end up worse than Daddy—because
I wouldn't be doing what I know I got to do—I *got* to
do! I've seen your life—and now I see Daddy—and I
love you, I love you both!—but I've got my work to do,
something's happening in the world out there, I got to
go! I know you think I don't know what's happening,
but I'm beginning to see—something. Every time I
play, every time I listen, I see Daddy's face and yours,

and so many faces—who's going to speak for all that, Mama? Who's going to speak for all of us? I can't stay home. Maybe I can say something—one day—maybe I can say something in music that's never been said before. Mama—*you* knew this day was coming.

MARGARET: I reckon I thought I was Joshua and could make the sun stand still.

DAVID: Mama, I'm leaving this house tonight. I'm going on the road with some other guys. I got a lot of things to do today and I ain't going to be hanging around the house. I'll see you before I go.

(He starts for the door.)

MARGARET: David—?

DAVID: Yes, Mama?

MARGARET: Don't you want to eat something?

DAVID: No, Mama. I ain't hungry now.

(He goes.)

MARGARET: Well. There he go. Who'd ever want to love a man and raise a child! Odessa—you think I'm a hard woman?

ODESSA: No. I don't think you a hard woman. But I think you's in a hard place.

MARGARET: I done something, somewhere, wrong.

ODESSA: Remember this morning. You got a awful thing ahead of you this morning. You got to go upstairs and win them folks back to you this morning.

MARGARET: My man is in there, dying, and my baby's in the world—how'm I going to preach, Odessa? How'm I going to preach when I can't even pray?

ODESSA: You got to face them. You got to think. You got to pray.

MARGARET: Sister, I can't. I can't. I can't.

ODESSA: Maggie. It was you had the vision. It weren't me. You got to think back to the vision. If the vision was for anything, it was for just this day.

MARGARET: The vision. Ah, it weren't yesterday, that vision. I was in a cold, dark place and I thought it was the grave. And I listened to hear my little baby cry and didn't no cry come. I heard a voice say, Maggie. Maggie. You got to find you a hiding place. I wanted Luke. *(She begins to weep.)* Oh, sister, I don't remember no vision. I just remember that it was dark and I was scared and my baby was dead and I wanted Luke, I wanted Luke, I wanted Luke!

ODESSA: Oh, honey. Oh, my honey. What we going to do with you this morning? *(MARGARET cannot stop weeping.)* Come on, honey, come on. You got them folks to face.

MARGARET: All these years I prayed as hard as I knowed how. I tried to put my treasure in heaven where couldn't nothing get at it and take it away from me and leave me alone. I asked the Lord to hold my hand. I didn't expect that none of this would ever rise to hurt me no more. And all these years it just been waiting for me, waiting for me to turn a corner. And there it stand, my whole life, just like I hadn't never gone nowhere. It's a awful thing to think about, the way love never dies!

ODESSA: You's got to pull yourself together and think how you can *win*. You always been the winner. Ain't no time to be a woman *now*. You can't let them throw you out of this church. What we going to do then? I'm getting old, I can't help you. And you ain't young no more, neither.

MARGARET: Maybe we could go—someplace else.

ODESSA: We ain't got no money to go no place. We ain't paid the rent for this month. We ain't even finished paying for this Frigidaire.

MARGARET: I remember in the old days whenever Luke wanted to spend some money on foolishness, that is exactly what I would have to say to him: "Man, ain't you got good sense? Do you know we ain't even paid the rent for this month?"

ODESSA: Margaret. You got to think.

MARGARET: Odessa, you remember when we was little there was a old blind woman lived down the road from us. She used to live in this house all by herself and you used to take me by the hand when we walked past her house because I was scared of her. I can see her, just as plain somehow, sitting on the porch, rocking in that chair, just looking out over them roads like she could see something. And she used to hear us coming, I guess, and she'd shout out, "How you this Lord's-day morning?" Don't care what day it was, or what time of day it was, it was always the Lord's-day morning for her. Daddy used to joke about her, he used to say, "Ain't no man in that house. It's a mighty sad house." I reckon this going to be a mighty sad house before long.

ODESSA: Margaret. You got to think.

MARGARET: I'm thinking. I'm thinking. I'm thinking how I throwed away my life.

ODESSA: You can't think about it like that. You got to remember—you gave your life to the Lord.

MARGARET: I'm thinking now—maybe Luke needed it more. Maybe David could of used it better. I know. I got to go upstairs and face them people. Ain't nothing else left for me to do. I'd like to talk to Luke.

ODESSA: I'll go on up there.

MARGARET: The only thing my mother should have told me is that being a woman ain't nothing but one long fight with men. And even the Lord, look like, ain't nothing but the most impossible kind of man there is. Go on upstairs, sister. Be there—when I get there.

(After a moment, ODESSA goes. Again, we hear the sound of singing: "God be with you till we meet again."

MARGARET *walks into* LUKE's *bedroom, stands there a moment, watching him.*

BROTHER BOXER *enters the kitchen, goes to the Frigidaire, pours himself a Kool-Aid.)*

MARGARET *(Turns)*: What are you doing down here, Brother Boxer? Why ain't you upstairs in the service?

BROTHER BOXER: Why ain't *you* upstairs in the service, Sister Margaret? We's waiting for you upstairs.

MARGARET: I'm coming upstairs! Can't you go on back up there now and ask them folks to be—a little quiet? He's sick, Brother Boxer. He's sick!

BROTHER BOXER: You just finding that out? He *been* sick, Sister Margaret. How come it ain't never upset you until now? And how you expect me to go upstairs and ask them folks to be quiet when you been telling us all these years to praise the Lord with fervor? Listen! They got fervor. Where's all your fervor done gone to, Sister Margaret?

MARGARET: Brother Boxer, even if you don't want me for your pastor no more, please remember I'm a woman. Don't talk to me this way.

BROTHER BOXER: A woman? Is *that* where all your fervor done gone to? You trying to get back into that man's arms, Sister Margaret? What you want him to do for you—you want him to take off that long white robe?

MARGARET: Be careful, Brother Boxer. It ain't over yet. It ain't over yet.

BROTHER BOXER: Oh, yes it is, Sister Margaret. It's over. You just don't know it's over. Come on upstairs. Maybe you can make those folks keep quiet.

(The music has stopped.)

They's quiet now. They's waiting for you.

MARGARET: You hate me. How long have you hated me? What have I ever done to make you hate me?

BROTHER BOXER: All these years you been talking about how the Lord done called you. Well, you sure come running but I ain't so sure you was called. I seen you in there, staring at that man. You ain't no better than the rest of them. You done sweated and cried in the nighttime, too, and you'd like to be doing it again. You had me fooled with that long white robe but you ain't no better. You ain't as good. You been sashaying around here acting like weren't nobody good enough to touch the hem of your garment. You was always so pure, Sister Margaret, you made the rest of us feel like dirt.

MARGARET: I was trying to please the Lord.

BROTHER BOXER: And you reckon you did? Declare, I never thought I'd see you so quiet. All these years I been running errands for you, saying, Praise the Lord, Sister Margaret. That's *right,* Sister Margaret! Amen, Sister Margaret! I didn't know if you even knew what a man was. I never thought I'd live long enough to find out that Sister Margaret weren't nothing but a woman who run off from her husband and then started ruling other people's lives because she didn't have no man to control her. I sure hope you make it into heaven, girl. You's too late to catch any other train.

MARGARET: It's not over yet. It's not over.

BROTHER BOXER: You coming upstairs?

MARGARET: I'm coming.

BROTHER BOXER: Well. We be waiting.

(He goes. MARGARET *stands alone in the kitchen. As* BROTHER BOXER *enters, the lights in the church go up. The church is packed. Far in the back* SISTER ODESSA *sits.* SISTER MOORE *is in the pulpit, and a baritone soloist is singing.)*

BARITONE:

Soon I'll be done with the troubles of the world,
Troubles of the world, troubles of the world,
Soon I'll be done with the troubles of the world,
Going home to live with my Lord.

Soon I'll be done with the troubles of the world,
Troubles of the world, troubles of the world,
Soon I'll be done with the troubles of the world,
Going home to live with my Lord.

Soon I'll be done with the troubles of the world,
Troubles of the world, troubles of the world,
Soon I'll be done with the troubles of the world,
Going home to live with my Lord.

SISTER MOORE *(Reads)*: For if after they have escaped the pollution of the world through the knowledge of the Lord and Saviour Jesus Christ they are again entangled therein and overcome, the latter end is worse with them than the beginning.

ALL: Amen!

SISTER MOORE *(Reads)*: For it had been better for them not to have known the way of righteousness than after they had known it to turn away from the holy commandment delivered unto them. Amen! Sister Boxer, would you read the last verse for us? Bless our God!

SISTER BOXER *(Reads)*: But it is happened unto them according to the true proverb, the dog is turned to his own vomit again and the sow that was washed to her wallowing in the mire.

(The church dims out. MARGARET *walks into the bedroom.)*

MARGARET: Luke?

LUKE: Maggie. Where's my son?

MARGARET: He's gone, Luke. I couldn't hold him. He's gone off into the world.

LUKE: He's gone?

MARGARET: He's gone.

LUKE: He's gone into the world. He's into the world!

MARGARET: Luke, you won't never see your son no more.

LUKE: But I seen him one last time. He's in the world, he's living.

MARGARET: He's gone. Away from you and away from me.

LUKE: He's living. He's living. Is you got to see your God to know he's living.

MARGARET: Everything—is dark this morning.

LUKE: You all in white. Like you was the day we got married. You mighty pretty.

MARGARET: It were a sunny day. Like today.

LUKE: Yeah. They used to say, "Happy is the bride the sun shines on."

MARGARET: Yes. That's what they used to say.

LUKE: Was you happy that day, Maggie?

MARGARET: Yes.

LUKE: I loved you, Maggie.

MARGARET: I know you did.

LUKE: I love you still.

MARGARET: I know you do.

(They embrace and singing is heard from the darkened church: "The Old Ship of Zion.")

Maybe it's not possible to stop loving anybody you ever really loved. I never stopped loving you, Luke. I tried. But I never stopped loving you.

LUKE: I'm glad you's come back to me, Maggie. When your arms was around me I was always safe and happy.

MARGARET: Oh, Luke! If we could only start again!

(His mouthpiece falls from his hand to the floor.)

Luke?

(He does not answer.)

My baby. You done joined hands with the darkness.

(She rises, moving to the foot of the bed, her eyes on LUKE. She sees the mouthpiece, picks it up, looks at it.)

My Lord! If I could only start again! If I could only start again!

(The light comes up in the church. All, except ODESSA, are

singing, "I'm Gonna Sit at the Welcome Table," clapping, etc. SISTER MOORE *leads the service from the pulpit. Still holding* LUKE's *mouthpiece clenched against her breast,* MARGARET *mounts into the church. As she enters, the music dies.)*

MARGARET: Praise the Lord!

SISTER MOORE: You be careful, Sister Margaret. Be careful what you say. You been uncovered.

MARGARET: I come up here to put you children on your knees! Don't you know the Lord is displeased with every one of you? Have every one of you forgot your salvation? Don't you know that it is *forbidden*—amen!—to talk against the Lord's anointed? Ain't a soul under the sound of my voice—bless God!—who has the right to sit in judgment on my life! Sister Margaret, this woman you see before you, has given her life to the Lord—and you say the Lord is displeased with me because ain't a one of you willing to endure what I've endured. Ain't a one of you willing to go—the road I've walked. This way of holiness ain't no joke. You can't love the Lord and flirt with the Devil. The Word of God is right and the Word of God is plain—and you can't love God unless you's willing to give up everything for Him. Everything. I want you folks to pray. I want every one of you to go down on your knees. We going to have a tarry service here tonight. Oh, yes! David, you play something on that piano—
(*She stops, stares at the piano, where one of the saints from Philadelphia is sitting.*)

David—David—

(She looks down at her fist.)

Oh, my God.

SISTER BOXER: Look at her! *Look* at her! The gift of God has left her!

MARGARET: Children. I'm just now finding out what it means to love the Lord. It ain't all in the singing and the shouting. It ain't all in the reading of the Bible. *(She unclenches her fist a little.)* It ain't even—it ain't even—in running all over everybody trying to get to heaven. To love the Lord is to love all His children—all of them, everyone!—and suffer with them and rejoice with them and never count the cost!

(Silence. She turns and leaves the pulpit.)

SISTER MOORE: Bless our God! He give us the victory! I'm gonna feast on milk and honey.

(She is joined by the entire congregation in this final song of jubilation.

MARGARET *comes down the stairs. She stands in the kitchen.*

ODESSA *comes downstairs. Without a word to* MARGARET, *she goes through* LUKE'S *room, taking off her robe as she goes. The lights dim down in the church, dim up on* MARGARET, *as* MARGARET *starts toward the bedroom, and falls beside* LUKE'S *bed. The scrim comes down. One or two people pass in the street.)*

CURTAIN

END OF ACT THREE

THE DISCOVERY OF WHAT IT MEANS
TO BE AN AMERICAN

"It is a complex fate to be an American," Henry James observed, and the principal discovery an American writer makes in Europe is just how complex this fate is. America's history, her aspirations, her peculiar triumphs, her even more peculiar defeats, and her position in the world—yesterday and today—are all so profoundly and stubbornly unique that the very word "America" remains a new, almost completely undefined and extremely controversial proper noun. No one in the world seems to know exactly what it describes, not even we motley millions who call ourselves Americans.

I left America because I doubted my ability to survive the fury of the color problem here. (Sometimes I still do.) I wanted to prevent myself from becoming *merely* a Negro; or, even, merely a Negro writer. I wanted to find out in what way the *specialness* of my experience could be made to connect me with other people instead of dividing me from them. (I was as isolated from Negroes as I was from whites, which is what happens when a Negro begins, at bottom, to believe what white people say about him.)

In my necessity to find the terms on which my experience could be related to that of others, Negroes and whites, writers and non-writers, I proved, to my astonishment, to be as American as any Texas G.I. And I found my experience was shared by every American writer I knew in Paris. Like me, they had been divorced from their origins, and it turned out to make very little difference that the origins of white Americans were European and mine were African— they were no more at home in Europe than I was.

The fact that I was the son of a slave and they were the sons of free men meant less, by the time we confronted each other on European soil, than the fact that we were both searching for our separate identities. When we had found these, we seemed to be saying, why, then, we would no longer need to cling to the shame and bitterness which had divided us so long.

It became terribly clear in Europe, as it never had been here, that we knew more about each other than any European ever could. And it also became clear that, no matter where our fathers had been born, or what they had endured, the fact of Europe had formed us both was part of our identity and part of our inheritance.

I had been in Paris a couple of years before any of this became clear to me. When it did, I, like many a writer before me upon the discovery that his props have all been knocked out from under him, suffered a species of breakdown and was carried off to the mountains of Switzerland. There, in that absolutely alabaster landscape, armed with two Bessie Smith records and a typewriter, I began to try to re-create the life that I had first known as a child and from which I had spent so many years in flight.

It was Bessie Smith, through her tone and her cadence, who helped me to dig back to the way I myself must have spoken when I was a pickaninny, and to remember the things I had heard and seen and felt. I had buried them very deep. I had never listened to Bessie Smith in America (in the same way that, for years, I would not touch watermelon), but in Europe she helped to reconcile me to being a "nigger."

I do not think that I could have made this reconciliation here. Once I was able to accept my role—as distinguished, I must say, from my "place"—in the extraordinary drama which is America, I was released from the illusion that I hated America.

The story of what can happen to an American Negro

writer in Europe simply illustrates, in some relief, what can happen to any American writer there. It is not meant, of course, to imply that it happens to them all, for Europe can be very crippling, too; and, anyway, a writer, when he has made his first breakthrough, has simply won a crucial skirmish in a dangerous, unending and unpredictable battle. Still, the breakthrough is important, and the point is that an American writer, in order to achieve it, very often has to leave this country.

The American writer, in Europe, is released, first of all, from the necessity of apologizing for himself. It is not until he *is* released from the habit of flexing his muscles and proving that he is just a "regular guy" that he realizes how crippling this habit has been. It is not necessary for him, there, to pretend to be something he is not, for the artist does not encounter in Europe the same suspicion he encounters here. Whatever the Europeans may actually think of artists, they have killed enough of them off by now to know that they are as real—and as persistent—as rain, snow, taxes, or businessmen.

Of course, the reason for Europe's comparative clarity concerning the different functions of men in society is that European society has always been divided into classes in a way that American society never has been. A European writer considers himself to be part of an old and honorable tradition—of intellectual activity, of letters—and his choice of a vocation does not cause him any uneasy wonder as to whether or not it will cost him all his friends. But this tradition does not exist in America.

On the contrary, we have a very deep-seated distrust of real intellectual effort (probably because we suspect that it will destroy, as I hope it does, that myth of America to which we cling so desperately). An American writer fights his way to one of the lowest rungs on the American social ladder by means of pure bull-headedness and an indescribable series of odd jobs. He probably *has* been a "regular fellow" for much of his adult life, and it is not easy for him to step out of that lukewarm bath.

We must, however, consider a rather serious paradox: though American society is more mobile than Europe's, it is easier to cut across social and occupational lines there than it is here. This has something to do, I think, with the problem of status in American life. Where everyone has status, it is also perfectly possible, after all, that no one has. It seems inevitable, in any case, that a man may become uneasy as to just what his status is.

But Europeans have lived with the idea of status for a long time. A man can be as proud of being a good waiter as of being a good actor, and, in neither case, feel threatened. And this means that the actor and the waiter can have a freer and more genuinely friendly relationship in Europe than they are likely to have here. The waiter does not feel, with obscure resentment, that the actor has "made it," and the actor is not tormented by the fear that he may find himself, tomorrow, once again a waiter.

This lack of what may roughly be called social paranoia causes the American writer in Europe to feel—almost certainly for the first time in his life—that he can reach out to everyone, that he is accessible to everyone and open to everything. This is an extraordinary feeling. He feels, so to speak, his own weight, his own value.

It is as though he suddenly came out of a dark tunnel and found himself beneath the open sky. And, in fact, in Paris, I began to see the sky for what seemed to be the first time. It was borne in on me—and it did not make me feel melancholy—that this sky had been there before I was born and would be there when I was dead. And it was up to me, therefore, to make of my brief opportunity the most that could be made.

I was born in New York, but have lived only in pockets of it. In Paris, I lived in all parts of the city—on the Right Bank and the Left, among the bourgeoisie and among *les misérables,* and knew all kinds of people, from pimps and prostitutes in Pigalle to Egyptian bankers in Neuilly. This may sound extremely unprincipled or even obscurely immoral: I found it healthy. I love to talk to people, all kinds of people, and almost everyone, as I hope we still know, loves a man who loves to listen.

This perpetual dealing with people very different from

myself caused a shattering in me of preconceptions I scarcely knew I held. The writer is meeting in Europe people who are not American, whose sense of reality is entirely different from his own. They may love or hate or admire or fear or envy this country—they see it, in any case, from another point of view, and this forces the writer to reconsider many things he had always taken for granted. This reassessment, which can be very painful, is also very valuable.

This freedom, like all freedom, has its dangers and its responsibilities. One day it begins to be borne in on the writer, and with great force, that he is living in Europe as an American. If he were living there as a European, he would be living on a different and far less attractive continent.

This crucial day may be the day on which an Algerian taxi driver tells him how it feels to be an Algerian in Paris. It may be the day on which he passes a café terrace and catches a glimpse of the tense, intelligent, and troubled face of Albert Camus. Or it may be the day on which someone asks him to explain Little Rock and he begins to feel that it would be simpler—and, corny as the words may sound, more honorable—to *go* to Little Rock than sit in Europe, on an American passport, trying to explain it.

This is a personal day, a terrible day, the day to which his entire sojourn has been tending. It is the day he realizes that there are no untroubled countries in this fearfully troubled world; that if he has been preparing himself for anything in Europe, he has been preparing himself—for America. In short, the freedom that the American writer finds in Europe brings him, full circle, back to himself, with the responsibility for his development where it always was: in his own hands.

Even the most incorrigible maverick has to be born somewhere. He may leave the group that produced him—he may be forced to—but nothing will efface his origins, the marks of which he carries with him everywhere. I think it is important to know this and even find it a matter for rejoicing, as the strongest people do, regardless of their station. On this acceptance, literally, the life of a writer depends.

The charge has often been made against American writers that they do not describe society, and have no interest in it. They only describe individuals in opposition to it, or isolated from it. Of course, what the American writer is describing is his own situation. But what is *Anna Karenina* describing if not the tragic fate of the isolated individual, at odds with her time and place?

The real difference is that Tolstoy was describing an old and dense society in which everything seemed—to the people in it, though not to Tolstoy—to be fixed forever.

And the book is a masterpiece because Tolstoy was able to fathom, and make us see, the hidden laws which really governed this society and made Anna's doom inevitable.

American writers do not have a fixed society to describe. The only society they know is one in which nothing is fixed and in which the individual must fight for his identity. This is a rich confusion, indeed, and it creates for the American writer unprecedented opportunities.

That the tensions of American life, as well as the possibilities, are tremendous is certainly not even a question. But these are dealt with in contemporary literature mainly compulsively; that is, the book is more likely to be a symptom of our tension than an examination of it. The time has come, God knows, for us to examine ourselves, but we can only do this if we are willing to free ourselves of the myth of America and try to find out what is really happening here.

Every society is really governed by hidden laws, by unspoken but profound assumptions on the part of the people, and ours is no exception. It is up to the American writer to find out what these laws and assumptions are. In a society much given to smashing taboos without thereby managing to be liberated from them, it will be no easy matter.

It is no wonder, in the meantime, that the American writer keeps running off to Europe. He needs sustenance for his journey and the best models he can find. Europe has what we do not have yet, a sense of the mysterious and inexorable limits of life, a sense, in a word, of tragedy. And we have what they sorely need: a new sense of life's possibilities.

In this endeavor to wed the vision of the Old World with that of the New, it is the writer, not the statesman, who is our strongest arm. Though we do not wholly believe it yet, the interior life is a real life, and the intangible dreams of people have a tangible effect on the world.

VINTAGE BOOKS BY JAMES BALDWIN

Another Country

Set in Greenwich Village, Harlem, and France, *Another Country* is a novel depicting men and women, blacks and whites, stripped of their masks of gender and race by passion at its most elemental and sublime.

Fiction/Literature/0-679-74471-1

The Fire Next Time

A classic work of the African–American experience—at once a powerful evocation of Baldwin's childhood in Harlem and a disturbing examination of the consequences of racial injustice.

Literature/African-American Studies/0-679-74472-X

Nobody Knows My Name

A collection of provocative essays on race relations in the United States, incisive meditations on the problem of individual identity, cogent discussions of the writer's place in society, and more.

Literature/African-American Studies/0-679-74473-8

Blues for Mister Charlie

From the murder that marks its opening scene to the scathing dialogue that renders racism in America as a palpable emotion that grips the heart, this award-winning play is contemporary drama at its best.

Drama/Literature/0-679-76178-0

Going to Meet the Man

A collection of eight short stories that explore, with devastating frankness, the roots of love, hate, and racial conflict.

Fiction/Literature/0-679-76179-9

The Amen Corner

Baldwin's first work for the theater, *The Amen Corner* is a play about faith and family, about the gulf between black men and black women and black fathers and black sons.

Drama/0-375-70188-5

Tell Me How Long the Train's Been Gone

In this intensely felt novel, an actor at the height of his theatrical career is nearly felled by a heart attack. As he hovers between life and death, the choices that have made him enviably famous and terrifyingly vulnerable are revealed.

Fiction/Literature/0-375-70189-3

Printed in the United States
by Baker & Taylor Publisher Services